She turned her face and smiled up at him in the shadowy carriage.

"What are you doing, Eduardo?" Her face was a pale heart, with a gleam of dark eyes and a flash of white teeth.

He watched a moment, entranced; then his head lowered and his lips touched her eyes. "Trying to ease your migraine," he said. His voice sounded husky.

She continued gazing at him while her lips formed a soft smile. "It feels good. Don't stop."

A warm breath fanned his cheek. At this close range, he noticed some exotic perfume escaping from her curls. He remembered her dance and felt that tingling excitement stir again within him. "Helena, darling . . ." His lips seized hers, and when she did not pull away, they firmed for a kiss. . . .

THE
SPANISH
LADY

Joan Smith

FAWCETT CREST • NEW YORK

A Fawcett Crest Book
Published by Ballantine Books
Copyright © 1992 by Joan Smith

All rights reserved under International and Pan-American Copyright Conventions. Published in the United States by Ballantine Books Inc., a division of Random House, Inc., New York, and simultaneously in Canada by Random House of Canada Limited, Toronto.

Library of Congress Catalog Card Number: 92-97055

ISBN 0-449-22141-5

Manufactured in the United States of America

First Edition: January 1993

Chapter One

Lady Hadley felt a disquieting tension in the elegant Gold Saloon on Belgrave Square. At two and fifty, her beauty had dwindled to a memory. Her golden hair was fast fading to silver, and her rosepetal cheeks were becoming sere, but some remnants of beauty lingered in her vacuous blue eyes. She watched as her son shredded a perfectly harmless letter to bits of paper and dropped the pieces like snowflakes onto the sofa table. Her son seemed tense today, too. She could not imagine why Edward should be wearing a Friday face, with the pleasures of the Season about to begin.

He had been in the mopes ever since their arrival in London last week. Perhaps it had been a mistake to come early, but she was always eager to escape from her husband. Hadley, of course, had no use for London. He much preferred the company of his cattle to that of society.

"I say, Edward," she said to cheer him up, "you have not forgotten Cousin Algernon's daughter will be arriving one of these days? Papa wanted you to arrange for meeting her."

Strangely, this remark only tightened the thin line of Lord Severn's lips. She wished he would not do that—so unattractive. She puckered her brow

1

and thought a moment, then said, "How will we know when to expect her? It is not as though she were coming on a stagecoach from Brighton or Bath. A ship coming all the way from Spain might be *hours* late."

"It might be days or even weeks late, Mama," Severn pointed out. To himself he added, With luck, she may not come at all. A squall at sea, perhaps, would be his salvation.

It was hard to believe this wide-shouldered, six-foot-tall gentleman with hair as black as jet was Lady Hadley's son. The only similarity was in the conformation of the eyes: they had the same deep blue eyes, with a sweep of sooty lashes. In Severn's case, however, the vacuity was replaced by an intelligent twinkle.

Lady Hadley said, "*Days!* Good gracious! The poor people waiting for it to land—I hope they take food, and perhaps even a pillow and blanket. But you forget, my dear, did your papa not say something about the Admiralty having scouts on the lookout for ships coming in? You were to ask to be notified when the *Princess Maria* was spotted. We would not want Lady Helena to land all alone in a foreign country."

Lord Severn wished with all his heart she would not land at all. His father's injunctions rang in his ears. "Thirty years is plenty long enough to fritter away your time. As you cannot find a bride to suit you in England, I have invited Lord Aylesbury to send his daughter to us. Try if you can get her shackled before she discovers what a useless fellow you are."

"It seems odd to have a goddaughter I have never laid an eye on," Lady Hadley said. "I was godmama to my cousin Algernon's daughter by what they call proxy, since Algernon wanted her to have *one* English godparent, at least, and it is well he did so, for now, you see . . ." She stumbled to a stop to collect her wits and try again.

"What I mean is, with the Frenchies rampaging through the Peninsula, it is well that Lady Helena has me to come to, or what would happen to her? Algernon is remaining in Spain, and her mama is dead, so, really, I don't know what the poor child could have done if I had not taken her."

"She must have other relatives. Has Algernon no sisters or brothers?" Severn asked.

"To be sure, my dear, Lancashire is full of them, but how should poor Helena make her bows from Lancashire? She is a great heiress, you must know. Her grandpapa on her mama's side was a *conde*, which is a sort of foreign lord, which is why Algernon is remaining in Spain, to try to fight Napoléon's army and help to save the family fortune. His bride brought him a splendid vineyard as her dowry. Or perhaps he is going to be a spy, or something exciting, for he was the only one of the Carlisles who ever had an ounce of spunk. Fancy his going to Spain in the first place."

"Fancy his not knowing enough to come home when war threatened," Severn murmured. As his mama had not mentioned the plan of marrying Lady Helena, Severn assumed she had not been told of it. Papa never told her anything. He treated her like a child.

"Have you entered Lady Helena's name for presentation at court, Mama?" he asked.

"Ninnyhammer. It was the first thing I did upon reaching London. Cousin Audrey and I have been

3

as close as inkle weavers all week, preparing for her debut. Cousin Audrey has brought Marion to town again this spring for another try. Poor girl. She is getting a tad long in the tooth, but her uncle Rochester recently left her five thousand, and with her own five thousand, it may be enough to tempt someone into an offer."

"I doubt it," Severn said bluntly.

"So do I. But in any case, Audrey has offered to help us chaperon Helena. I am getting pretty old to be trotting every evening, but you and Audrey can help me keep an eye on her."

This brought a spark of pleasure to Severn's jaded eyes. He was happy Lady Helena's friends had not been chosen from his own circle. The Comstocks would steer Lady Helena to concerts of ancient music and dull tea parties, leaving him free for more dashing entertainments.

"An excellent notion, Mama."

"Yes, and Lady Helena will get on with them like a house on fire. She is bound to be a well-behaved girl. I do not look for any mischief in her. She was reared in the strictest circumstances. In fact, she spent considerable time in a convent when the fighting came close to her home. Apparently the convents were safe. Algernon never said so, but I suspect his wife was a papist. Spain is riddled with them," she confided. "I cannot think why the Court allows it."

Severn opened his lips but was daunted by the chore of explaining hundreds of years of history, and closed them again. "She speaks English, doesn't she?"

"She does, but she would be accustomed to speaking Spanish in the convent, so I daresay she will be

4

a little shy of English strangers. You must try to bring her out a little, Severn. The poor girl is bound to be ugly. Algernon had a face like a cod's head, and her mama, you recall, was a foreigner."

This was the first time his mama had seen fit to mention the girl's appearance. Severn felt his interest, which had been tweaked by her romantic background, shrivel. "We must be thankful for the dowry," he said, and turned to that part of the journal dealing with the race course.

Aboard the *Princess Maria*, Lady Helena sat tapping her foot and gazing at an ivory miniature of Lord Severn. Its arrival had caused a small spark of interest in this English cousin Papa wished her to marry. He was handsome, but she was not fool enough to fall in love with a picture. Especially if this was how Lord Severn planned to treat her! He ought to have been waiting at the dock with a carriage. She had told Papa frankly she had no intention of having her husband chosen for her. She would go to England—it sounded a pleasant adventure—but if she married, it would be to a man of her own choosing. Papa was not brave, or foolish, enough to command his headstrong daughter.

Her pride disliked to send to Belgrave Square begging for a carriage. It was not to be thought of. She summoned a servant and asked to have a hansom cab sent to her. Within minutes, she was traveling through London—a poor, shabby sort of place it looked, although it improved greatly when they reached the West End. Still, the red brick house at which the carriage stopped was but a cottage compared to Papa's Viñedo Paraíso, in Jerez.

The sound of the door knocker echoed faintly in

Lady Hadley's saloon. "That will be Audrey, I expect," she said. "She often drops in after shopping." She waited for the butler to announce Mrs. Comstock. The faint knock was repeated.

"Sugden has either dozed off or abandoned his post," Severn scolded.

"No, it is his bad tooth. He has been dosing himself with oil of cinnamon. I told him he must have the tooth drawn. Take Audrey to my parlor, Edward. It has a fire laid. I shall ask for fresh tea and meet her there."

Severn strode to the front door and threw it open. He found himself staring at a female who looked as if she belonged on the stage, perhaps playing a gypsy. Her raven hair was drawn back under a fashionable bonnet, beneath whose brim a pair of darkly flashing eyes examined him boldly. Her pale face was heart-shaped and pretty. For the rest, he had an impression of an outfit of some strange cut and garish scarlet color.

"I would like to see Lady Hadley," the apparition announced, and stepped forward.

Severn blocked the doorway with his body. His mama was enjoying a surfeit of callers this season, with a deb to be sponsored. This one looked like a modiste, or milliner, or perhaps even a coiffeuse. Stylish but not quite a lady, was his estimate. "Use the back door next time, miss," he said, "but since you are here, I shall see if Lady Hadley can spare you a moment."

Lady Helena came in and turned an imperious eye on him. She had been gazing at a likeness of that arrogant face for the past half hour. She had to find her own way to Belgrave Square, and now this insult! *Use the back door.* It was not to be borne.

If he mistook her for a servant, she would return the compliment.

Without a word, she removed her bonnet and handed it to him. "I am Señorita Helena Consuela Maria Elizabeth Carlisle, *idiota*. Lady Hadley is expecting me."

Severn stared in bewilderment. Her accent was quite pronounced, and as she spoke quickly, he caught only an occasional word. "What?" he asked, blinking.

"*¡Caracoles!*" she exclaimed, tossing up her hands. "Your mistress, *por favor.*"

"Good God!" he said, staring. What was this talk of his mistress? Was one of his friends playing a joke on him, sending a lightskirt to cause mischief? "Look here, miss," he said. "You'd best leave at—did you say Carlisle?"

"But yes. Señorita Carlisle, from España, to see your mistress, Lady Hadley. Bah, *no importa.* I shall discover her for myself," she said, and strode briskly down the hall.

Severn followed behind, carrying her bonnet, with a long black feather tipping over the brim.

Lady Hadley, curious at the delay, rose and went to the door of her parlor. She saw the vision in red advancing, heard the rattle of a foreign tongue, not French, and looked to Severn for elucidation.

"She has something to do with Lady Helena, I think," he said doubtfully. "A companion, perhaps, I wonder if the *Princess Maria* has arrived."

The visitor turned a sharp eye on him. How was it possible he did not know her ship had arrived? All the other important passengers had been met. "You are confused. I am who you call Lady Helena, but I do not call myself so. I am Señorita Carlisle.

My ship arrived many hours ago. I have waited and waited, until at last I could wait no longer and hired a carriage to come to you."

"You are Algernon Carlisle's daughter?" Lady Hadley asked, for it seemed entirely unlikely, unless Algernon had married a very beautiful giant. That seemed the sort of thing a man might have mentioned.

When Lady Helena turned to her godmother, all her anger melted at that welcoming smile. "Ah, *sí*, I am Papa's daughter, and you are Lady Hadley?"

"There is no question of *that*," the dame assured her.

"*¡Madrina!*" Lady Helena exclaimed, and rushed forward to pitch herself into Lady Hadley's arms. She towered a good six inches over her godmother, making the exercise a little precarious for the latter. Lady Hadley reeled backward, but Lady Helena steadied her, and with their arms interlocked, they walked toward the main saloon. Lady Hadley knew instinctively that her own small parlor would not do for this amazing lady. Severn followed them, still carrying the bonnet.

"I am curious why you call me *Madrina*, when you know my real name," Lady Hadley said, not in a condemning way, but as one seeking an answer.

"It means godmama."

"Really! Fancy that. I have been a *madrina* all the while and never knew it."

"One feels that ought to have been said in French." Severn smiled.

His mama frowned in perplexity. "Then it would not have been Spanish, would it, Edward?"

"No, it would have been Molière."

"Pay no heed to him. He has not been the same

8

since they published his letter to the editor in the *Morning Observer*," Lady Hadley said to her guest, and ushered her goddaughter into the Gold Saloon.

Lady Helena looked around at the opulence of Adam molding and matching marble fireplaces, at paintings by Gainsborough and Canaletto, at Persian carpets and graceful Hepplewhite settees and tables and said, "What a charming little house, *Madrina*. You must be quite cozy here." Then she removed her pelisse, handed it to Severn with a careless smile, and said, *"Gracias,"* with a dismissing flutter of her fingers. Severn took the pelisse and looked to the hall for Sugden.

"Would you please hang it up," Lady Helena said, patiently, as if he were an idiot, or perhaps deaf.

"Certainly," Severn said in momentary confusion, and took it into the hallway.

Lady Helena feared the butt of her joke was missing the whole point and said, "Is your *mayordomo loco, Madrina*?" This insult, she trusted, would work its way back to Severn's ears.

"I am afraid I don't speak Spanish, dear. Your papa told me you are quite good at English."

"Your serving man—butler?—is he crazy?"

"Sugden? Oh, no, my dear. He has an inflamed tooth. Where did you get the notion he is mad?"

"He tried to turn me away from your house. And then he told me I should go to the back door, if you please!"

"Really? I shall speak to him, depend upon it."

"I think you must."

Severn returned. "Your mistress has something to say to you, Sugden," Lady Helena said, with an encouraging look at her godmother.

Lady Hadley and her son exchanged a confused

glance. "This is my son, Edward," she said to their guest.

A flame of anger licked at Severn's breast. A butler! She had mistaken him for a *butler*! He observed the wisp of a smile Lady Helena could not control, and in an instant, he understood her ploy. She was repaying him for mistaking her for a servant. So the lady thought to retaliate, did she? If it was a duel of wits the lady desired, he felt he could accommodate her.

Severn performed a competent bow, while allowing his eyes to disparage every stitch on her body. "I pray you forgive my confusion, Lady Helena. We did not expect you to come by yourself. We were waiting to hear your ship had arrived, at which time we planned to thank your traveling companion and deliver you here."

"You are the Earl of Severn!" Lady Helena exclaimed. She rose and curtsied daintily, all the while returning Severn's examination. "The captain and his wife were my chaperons. They are good friends of Papa."

In Spain, ladies had very little to say about anything. It had been Lady Helena's custom to get what she wanted by winding her papa around her fingers. As this had proved so simple and expedient, she saw no reason to change her tactics in England. Lord Severn would rule the roost in this house; thus it was imperative that she bring him to heel. Fortunately, he was stupid. Also, he was not ugly. It was more amusing playing off one's stunts on a handsome gentleman.

"You must forgive me," she said, with a bashful sweep of her long lashes. "Papa did not tell me you were so handsome."

Severn, no stranger to ladies' wiles, knew a flirt when he saw one. When ladies pitched themselves at his head, it was usually in the hope of receiving an offer. Helena had come to England to nab him, but she would not find him an easy victim.

"How could he, when he has never seen me?" he replied indifferently.

"We had no idea you would be so pretty either, Lady Helena," Lady Hadley said. "I was just telling Edward, before you came, that you would probably be as ug—that is, you probably—"

"Mama thought you might favor your papa," Severn said.

"No, I am said to favor the Artolas—my mama's family," Helena replied. Then she added mischievously, "Though I ought to have recognized *you*, Lord Severn, for you somewhat resemble my papa." While she spoke, she noticed Severn's indifference to her insult. He was not offended, but he was not reacting to her as gentlemen usually did. Was he so slow, he responded to neither compliments nor insults?

Lady Hadley called for fresh tea, and for the next hour Lady Helena entertained her hosts with a lively description of her life in Spain and her trip. Lady Hadley wondered how it happened that they had not been notified of her ship's arrival, and after much discussion she decided that the Admiralty had forgotten to notify them. Severn sat like a mute. He had not bothered to speak to the Admiralty. It was the first step of his campaign to resist the marriage his father wanted.

"The captain told me I should have my trunks removed by tomorrow," Lady Helena said. "Can you arrange it for me, Lord Severn?"

"You had best see to it now, Edward," his mama said. "Helena will want to change for dinner."

"Yes, I should think so," he agreed at once, lifting a black arc of eyebrow at her brilliant gown.

"Perhaps if you could bring my bandbox with you," Lady Helena said, maintaining a smile in the teeth of this flagrant provocation.

Severn left at once, but his departure had more the air of an escape than that of dashing to do her bidding. He would require a little more butter before he was of the desired compliability.

Helena turned an imploring eye to her hostess. "Would it be possible, *Madrina*—a bath? The facilities on shipboard were primitive."

"I'll have hot water sent up to your room at once."

"Thank you. I shall soak until Severn brings my bandbox."

Before leaving the room, she placed a warm kiss on her godmother's cheek. "It is so very kind of you to have me. I think I am going to be very happy here. I shall try not to be a great nuisance, and if I do anything that displeases you, you must tell me at once. Agreed?"

"Of course, my dear, but I am sure you will behave very nicely. It will be like having a daughter at last."

They parted in perfect harmony.

Chapter Two

Lord Severn received another surprise when he inquired for Lady Helena's trunks at the ship. "Lady Helena Carlisle," he repeated, becoming impatient with the junior officer who assisted him. "She arrived this very day."

"Ah, you mean Señorita Carlisle, the Spanish lady! She asked us all to call her so," the junior officer explained. "Her trunks are ready and waiting. I promised her I'd attend to it personally."

He led Severn back to the gangplank and pointed to a small mountain of luggage already piled on a wagon. "There it is," he said. "The wagons come looking for work when a ship docks."

"Thank you," Severn said, and gave his address. "Lady Helena mentioned a bandbox she wished me to bring."

"I have that locked in my own cabin. I told her she should take it with her, but you know how much heed she pays to anyone. It was locked away, and she was eager to be off."

Severn frowned at this revelation of intimacy with the ship's officers. He got the bandbox and went to his carriage, determined to have a stern talk with Lady Helena before she was introduced to society. He returned at once to Belgrave Square with the bandbox and had it taken abovestairs. Of Lady Helena he saw not a trace for another four hours.

Her trunks arrived and were taken up to her. A servant unpacked while Helena oversaw the work. She rather enjoyed the interval. Since the French invasion of Spain, her life had been sorely unsettled. Although the war did not rage around Jerez, her papa had moved her many times; she had lived in castles and tents, in mansions and one convent, and it felt good to finally have a room—and a life— to call her own.

The good sisters would not be calling her to prayers at all hours of the day. No gunshots in the night to frighten the life out of one. No shortages of food. She would gladly have remained in Spain with her father, but he worried so. "Go home to England and enjoy your youth," Papa had said. "It comes only once, and it does not last long."

These rooms were the rooms to which she would return after her various rounds of pleasures. They were attractive, in a quiet way. Rooms in Spain were more highly garnished, usually with a deal of gold and red. The windows of her bedchamber and adjoining withdrawing room were hung in green damask. The walls bore nature scenes of birds and trees and flowers, delicately painted by hand on a fading cream background. A carved canopied bed dominated the bedchamber. It was dark and heavy. Helena felt she would spend more time in the little sitting room, with its grate, comfortable bergère chairs, and the dainty writing desk.

She had her stationery unpacked and arranged it in the cubbyholes of the desk. She would have to have new stationery printed, as the English, unlike

14

the Spanish, used a title for the children of their lords. Lady Helena, she would be called here. The English had a strange, harsh way of pronouncing it. At home, it was pronounced more fluidly: Aylehna.

Lying on top of her private stationery was a letter addressed simply to Moira. Moira, Señora Petrel-Jones, was Papa's lover. Helena knew that they had had an argument and Moira had left Spain. She had wanted to get a divorce and marry Papa, but he would not allow her to lower herself. It was uncertain that Helena would be able to deliver the letter. Papa had written it in the hope that she would find Moira when she reached London and eventually get the letter to her.

Spain was not so unnatural as to look down on a respectably married lady taking a lover, but a divorcée! It was not the thing. Word had leaked back to Spain that Mr. Petrel-Jones had died, so now the coast was clear for Moira and Papa to marry. The letter was an offer of marriage, begging Moira to return. Helena would make every effort to deliver it, for Papa would be lonesome now, with his daughter gone.

There was a tap at the door, and Lady Hadley peeped her head in. "It is only I, Helena," she said. "You will need someone to help you dress for dinner. I suggest Sally. She does for me when my woman's arthritis is acting up."

"Is Sally the one with the *pecas*?" She rubbed her nose.

"You mean freckles? Yes, poor Sal is sadly afflicted with a bran face, but she is clever with hair."

"Excellent, *Madrina*. You will help me find servants, *sí*?"

"There is no need for that, my dear. Algernon sent me a great deal of money to cover any little extra expenses. You must use my servants. That is all taken care of."

"But no! Papa told me I must not be a burden to you. I shall require a groom as well, for I mean to set up my own carriage *en seguida*."

"I am not sure folks drive their carriages *en seguida* here, but if it is some new thing, Edward will know about it."

"It means right away. I must try to speak only English."

"That might be best, at least until I get the hang of Spanish," her godmother replied foolishly. "And meanwhile Sal will do for you. We dine at eight, my dear."

"So early?"

"Early?" Why, eight is pretty late. In the country, folks eat at six. But I see what it is. They go changing the time when you travel. I have heard of this trick before. So confusing. I don't know why they bother, but then if we all spoke the same language and had the same time, what would be the point of traveling?"

Helena blinked in surprise at this farrago of nonsense. It was becoming clear where Lord Severn had gotten his small brain. "I shall be downstairs at eight. Is it to be *grande toilette*, or only family?"

"We thought you might be fagged this evening and have not invited guests."

"That is very thoughtful. *Gracias, Madrina*."

"Do you know, Helena, I think I am learning this Spanish already. I know *gracias* means thank you, for I have heard it before somewhere or other, and now I know *madrina* means godmama. I shall speak it—*en seguida!*" she said, and smiled triumphantly.

"*¡Bueno!*"

When the unpacking was finished, Helena dismissed the other servant, keeping Sally behind. "You are to assist me with my toilette," she said, sitting before the mirror at her toilette table. "Lady Hadley says you are good with hair. I hope you can do something with mine." She removed half a dozen pins, and a cascade of sable hair fell in ripples to her shoulders.

"Lordy!" Sally exclaimed. "I never handled such a lot of hair as this before. It looks like a curtain."

"It is a great nuisance," Lady Helena said. "My papa liked it long, but now that I am in England I shall have it cut off."

Sally lifted the raven tresses. They rippled silkily through her fingers. "It seems a shame, though."

"*¡Caramba!* You speak like my papa. *No importa.* Tonight you have only to arrange it. You can do this?"

"I can pin it up, milady, if that's what you mean."

"*Exactamente.*"

Sal worked her wizardry on Helena's hair, and when it was twisted and coiled into elegance, Helena selected her gown, a shimmering emerald green with black lace. With it, she wore her mama's emerald necklace. The gown clung to her waist and billowed in folds below. The bodice revealed the swell of satiny bosoms.

No Spanish maiden would have been allowed to appear in public in such a gown. Like most of Helena's outfits, it had belonged to her mama. Dressmaking had ground to a virtual halt with the onset of the war, and a young girl rapidly outgrowing her

17

short gowns had to wear something. Helena realized it was daring, but then England was well known for its debauched morals, second only to France in that interesting respect.

She took a long look in her mirror before going below. She could wish for another two inches of material at the bodice of her gown, but overall, she knew she looked well. A pretty face covered a multitude of peccadilloes. She lifted her skirt and strode imperiously to the staircase.

"Like the Queen of Sheba" was the way Sal described her to her colleagues when she returned to the kitchen. "More gowns than Lettie Lade, and brighter in color, too, with sparklers to match each one. That lady will nab herself a royal prince."

"Like a pricey bit o' muslin" was Severn's first impression when he beheld this alleged deb floating down the grand staircase. If Queen Charlotte should see her now, she would never permit Lady Helena to make her bows.

As she descended toward him, Helena noticed that Severn was very interested in either her emeralds or her bosoms. When he raised his eyes, he saw her gazing at him with a tolerant but faintly derisive smile.

"Good evening, Lord Severn. I hope I am not late."

"Good evening, Lady Helena. It is well we are dining alone, for in England, debs wear white gowns—of modest cut," he added, with a last glance at her immodesty.

"White! But no! It is my very worstest color. My skin is white. I shall look"—she tossed up her hands—"bleached."

"You will look as a young lady should look."

She frowned and put her hand on his arm to be led to the saloon, where Lady Hadley was impatient to get at her mutton.

"Don't you look fine as a star, Helena," she smiled, taking Severn's other arm and drawing him toward the dining room. To Severn she whispered aside, "But *quite* inappropriate."

When they were seated, Helena said, "I must speak to your Queen Charlotte about these white dresses. She is conversable?"

"No, my dear, she ain't," Lady Hadley said baldly. "Nothing is more likely to throw old Charlotte into a pelter than any sign of frowardness. But as soon as you nab a fellow, you may wear your pretty colored gowns."

"Ah, then I can tolerate white for a few weeks," Helena said, and began spooning up her cream of leek soup. She tasted the bland liquid and frowned at it. "May I have the pepper, please?" she asked, and was handed the pepper. She shook until the surface of her bowl was black, then stirred the pepper in and ate without either complaint or any sign of pleasure.

"I have never had milk soup before," she said. "It has a light flavor of onion, I think?"

"Leek, actually," Lady Hadley said.

It was clear to the meanest intelligence that Lady Helena found all the food similarly unappetizing. She flavored it liberally with pepper and any condiment she could get her hands on, but still it all lacked spice. They discussed her trip and affairs in Spain until the dessert appeared. Lady Helena was happy to see a dish of rice, even if it was being served alone and after the meat. She looked in amazement as her hostess added milk and sugar to the dish.

"Oh, *Madrina*! You cannot mean to *eat* that!" she exclaimed.

"Lovely rice pudding? Of course I mean to eat it, my dear. What else does one do with it, pray?"

Severn was destroying his rice in the same way. Lady Helena lightly sprinkled hers with salt and found it, like the rest of the meal, nearly inedible. She must get down to the kitchen very soon and teach their cook how to prepare rice. One could survive on rice for weeks, if necessary.

She was not tardy to leave the table when Lady Hadley rose. "We shall leave Severn to his port," the dame said, and led Helena to the saloon. "Edward retains the male's privilege of taking his wine after the ladies leave, even when we two dine alone. He will join us in half an hour or so."

Lady Helena did not think he would wait quite that long to join them. The stiff-faced milord might pretend disapproval of her gown and her manner, but he was interested for all that. She would try to hint Lady Hadley to bed early, so that she might flirt Severn into a more acquiescent mood.

Chapter Three

It was not fifteen minutes before Lord Severn joined the ladies in front of the grate. This was sufficient time to review the situation and find his solution. Since Lady Helena was pretty, he would hint her into the proper English mold and find a match for her. Papa could not blame him if she refused to have him. He would have "done his best" and failed.

"You are fast this evening, Edward," his mama exclaimed.

"Lady Helena is fagged after her journey. I wished for a few moments of her company before she retired."

Lady Helena blinked to hear she was expected to be tired at nine-thirty. Her whole aim was to be obliging, however, and she throated a yawn behind her daintily raised hand.

"It was the sea air that made me sleepy," she said, for she did not want them to get the idea she always retired in the middle of the afternoon.

Lady Hadley spoke a little about the coming Season—the balls and routs, Almack's and riding, while Severn added several injunctions on propriety.

Helena listened to both with avid interest. "Papa expects me to make a grand match," she said, trust-

21

ing Severn did not consider himself to be so grand as she meant. "I understand England has some quaint customs about white gowns and debs not waltzing and such things. You need not fear that I shall disgrace you by any impropriety." She turned to Severn and continued, "Actually, this gown you dislike so much, Lord Severn, was my late mama's. It was impossible to get new gowns made up with Spain at war, so we made do with what was at hand. Calling attention to oneself by odd behavior is considered vulgar in Spain, too."

Severn smiled his approval. Her mama's gowns, of course! He ought to have thought of that. "It will be acceptable for you to wear your mama's gowns when we dine at home, *en famille*," he said leniently. "The gown is charming, but not comme il faut for a deb."

Helena gave him her most demure smile. "I would not want you to think I was fast, milord!"

A bewitching smile the girl had, with little dimples at the corners of her lips, but none in her cheeks. It would be no trouble to find her a *parti*. "Call me Edward. You are my cousin, after all."

"Is it proper for me to ask you to call me Helena, Eduardo?" she asked, looking at him from the corner of her black eyes.

Eduardo. Never had his name sounded so romantic, almost daring. "Certainly. I am your cousin, too."

"We are all cousins, ninnyhammer," Lady Hadley declared. "Now, what sort of *parti* do you think Algernon has in his mind, my dear? Did he mention any names?" Severn stiffened.

Helena observed it. Was he going to be jealous and possessive? She must dispel the idea that the match was settled. "No, for he is not at all au courant with the Season's *partis*, but he expects me to marry a great man."

Severn relaxed visibly. Not jealousy, then, she concluded. Was it possible he did not wish to marry her? Even after he had seen her?

Lady Hadley said, "There is young Mondeville. He will be a duke when his papa sticks his fork in the wall."

"Why wait for that?" Severn asked. "Rutledge is a duke already." And a good friend, although he would not like a wayward bride. The dashing bucks never did. Helena must be talked up to Rutledge as a model of propriety.

After a little more talk, Helena tried another yawn, hoping to induce sleepiness in her hostess—yawns were supposed to be contagious. But the only result of her efforts was a suggestion from Severn that she should run along to bed, to be prepared for an outing tomorrow.

"Yes, indeed, for I am most eager to see your London."

She placed a kiss on her godmother's cheek, curtsied to Severn, and tripped off.

"It will be no trouble shooting her off," Lady Severn said to her son. "She is pretty as well as sensible. And not blessing herself all the time either, like our Mollie O'Dowd, who helped in the nursery, used to do. Only, of course, Mollie was Irish."

"Yes, she will do," Severn allowed. He was now easy in his mind that Mama was unaware of the groom Papa had in mind. And Helena, apparently, had no particular interest in him either. This bee was only in his father's bonnet.

"A pity you got off on the wrong foot with her by

taking her shawl this afternoon, like a butler. First impressions last. She is very well to grass, you must know. The vinery will be hers."

"And Rutledge is fond of his sherry," Severn said.

"I was wondering if *you* might not make a stab at her, Edward."

"I?" He laughed merrily. "Even you, Mama, cannot be such a peagoose as to consider *me* a great man."

"You could be. Brougham is always after you to be more active in politics."

"He spoke to me about taking the post of chancellor of the exchequer—in the shadow cabinet, of course," he added. "He is laboring under the delusion that I share Papa's wise ways with money."

"It would please your papa if you would do it."

Severn considered this notion. Papa would be in a rare pelter when he learned of Helena's engagement to Rutledge, or someone. Taking a more active part at Whitehall might mitigate his wrath. "I told Brougham I would consider it. I shall talk to him soon."

"You really should, for if you do not plan to marry soon, you ought to do something other than whore around town with those rackety friends of yours."

"Language, Mama. Remember, we have a maiden in the house."

Lady Hadley smiled fondly. "Fancy you giving *me* a lecture on propriety, Edward. Is it possible you are achieving a sense of responsibility at last?"

"I hope I am not irresponsible!"

"I am sure Papa exaggerates, but if you are going to straighten up, Edward, why not take a shot at Helena? If you think you really have a chance with that Incomparable, naturally I shall do everything in my power to abet you."

"I trust I could make myself agreeable, if I felt so inclined," he said, miffed at her doubting his ability to accomplish it on his own. "She is not just my type, however. You know I always preferred blondes, like you, Mama."

Lady Hadley was easily diverted with this compliment.

Severn drew out his watch and said, "It is still early. I believe I shall go down to my club for a few hands of cards."

"I shall send Audrey off a note. Perhaps she and Marion would like to go out with Helena tomorrow."

Severn thought a moment, then said, "No, don't do it. I shall show our cousin the sights of London, Mama." Naturally he must make some token attempt to amuse her. His father would demand to know what he was doing. But he would take care to show her a demmed flat time.

She nodded slyly. "I see. I shan't say a word about scheming or abetting, but I shall be indisposed when she wants to go out. Now run along and try to enjoy yourself."

This injunction was about as necessary as telling the archbishop of Canterbury to say his prayers. Severn seldom failed to enjoy himself, at least when he was in London. With the Season not yet open, he would go to his club and begin inciting his friends to an interest in Helena.

"I have a charming cousin visiting for the Season. A dark-eyed señorita from Spain," he said to Rutledge, but the others were listening. "And I don't want you fellows cluttering up the saloon. I think I shall keep this one for myself." This, of course, was bound to bring them to Belgrave Square in flocks. He continued to elaborate on her accent, her gowns, her romantic past, living in a castle and a convent. "Something quite out of the ordinary," he said with a sigh.

"A little too far out of the ordinary for me," Rutledge said. "Shall we play cards?"

"I am happy to hear it," Severn said, as if satisfied. "Of course, I am no friend to marriage myself, but gentlemen in our position must have a wife to provide an heir, to run our house, and to display at public functions. Naturally the lady we choose must be suitable as to breeding and bring a reasonable fortune with her. Twenty-five thousand and a vinery in Jerez."

"What vinery?" Rutledge asked at once.

"It is called Viñedo Paraíso, I believe. Formerly owned by the Artolas."

"But they make excellent stuff!" Rutledge exclaimed. "The finest amontillado I've found, and a very decent sweet sherry as well. The amoroso is excellent."

"I prefer claret myself. Your deal, I think," Severn said. He had hooked his fish. He wouldn't work the line.

He won fifty guineas at cards and returned at three, to sleep the sound sleep of the winner. There was a gray drizzle at the window the next morning, but it did not dampen his spirits. Let the española get a taste of English "sunshine." A few weeks of it might be enough to send her back to Spain.

He was happy to see Helena wearing a sad face when he joined her at breakfast. "Good morning, Helena. I hope you slept well?"

"Fine, thank you, Eduardo. What miserable luck! It is pouring rain."

"Pouring? Why, this is nothing. Much better than our usual spring weather."

She stared. "You think *Madrina* will venture out in such weather?"

"Probably not, but I shall be honored to escort you, Cousin."

He watched, fascinated, as her frown vanished, to be replaced with a radiant smile. "How very kind you are, Eduardo!"

"It will be my pleasure," he said with a bow.

His eyes skimmed over her toilette. The gown was different from English ladies' gowns in some subtle way. Brighter, richer, but by no means lacking propriety as to cut.

With her outing assured, Lady Helena forced herself to eat the unappetizing breakfast in her dish. The toasted bread was tolerable. Not even an English chef could entirely destroy eggs, and she made her meal of these, washed down with tea. She heartily wished she might have a cup of coffee.

Lady Hadley soon joined them. Her son said, "As it is raining, Mama, I shall go with Cousin this morning."

"Have you forgotten, Edward? We decided that last—"

"Naturally you will not want to go out in the damp," he said, cutting her off.

Helena sat like a spy, listening and coming to her own conclusions. Severn was making a pitch to win her. She turned a smile on him. "It is very kind of you, for this outing is most important."

"Where is it you want to go, dear?" Lady Hadley asked. "Did you wish to go to church? We have services only on Sunday in England—along with a few special feast days."

"Oh, no! I can wait until Sunday for church."

"Did you want to meet some of the exiled Spanish nobles? We have a flock of them, scheming to oust the Frenchies off their throne. So encroaching of Bonaparte to make his brother king of Spain."

"I should like to meet them soon, but that can wait a little. I was speaking of toilette. It is important that I be elegant, *Madrina*, as I plan to move in the first circles. I must see what the ladies are wearing before I make any purchases, *no es verdad*?"

Lady Hadley ignored her charge's occasional foray into foreign gibberish and said, "Severn is the very one whose advice you want. He will know what pleases the gentlemen."

Heedless of her wishes, Severn planned to take her on a tour of his own devising, beginning with Westminster and including such famous spots as St. Paul's Cathedral, Exeter Exchange, with a nod to the wild animals and the mint, the various royal residences, and ending in Hyde Park, if the rain ceased. If that did not bore her to distraction, he would be surprised.

"Mama will take you shopping another time," he said.

"She did not say shopping, gudgeon," his mother said bluntly. "She just wants to see what the ladies are wearing. A drive along Bond Street will do. The sun will soon be out. It rains every day," she confided to Helena, "but not for very long, usually."

"Every day!" She tossed up her hands in dismay. "*¡Que lástima!* What I ought to buy is a dozen waterproof coats, *no es verdad*?"

"You were going to try to speak a little English, dear," her godmother reminded her. "It sounds so very odd to hear all that foreign gibberish, *n'est-ce-pas?*"

Severn welcomed the reminder until his foolish mama added her French note. He glanced to see if Helena had noticed it. Her lips were moving unsteadily. She peered across the table at him, and he found himself sharing this private joke.

"What does that *no es verdad* thing mean in English, my dear?" Lady Hadley asked. "I might as well brush up on my Spanish while we are at it."

"In English it means *n'est-ce pas, Madrina*," she replied daringly.

"Ah, that is interesting. I see one would have any number of occasions to say it in that case—*no es verdad?*" She laughed merrily at her wit. "I shall be parlaying Spanish in no time at this rate."

Severn hid his amusement behind his teacup. When he set the cup down, he said, "All set, Helena?"

Chapter Four

Although it was unlikely Mrs. Petrel-Jones would be spotted on her first foray into London, Helena put her father's billet-doux in the bottom of her reticule. She meant to take it with her everywhere and make inquiries among all the people she met. Someone was bound to know her, or know of her.

"What bonnet will you be wanting, milady?" Sal asked.

"I shall wear my second-best pelisse, as it is pouring rain. The navy-glazed straw goes with it, if you please."

"Lovely! You'll look all the crack in this one."

"All the crack? What a droll expression," Helena said, adjusting the bonnet at a daring angle over her left eye.

"How'd you keep your skin so white, milady, in the burning hot sun of Spain?"

"I didn't. I was ruddy when I left. I spent much time below deck during the voyage, and my *pe*—my freckles faded. It is the sun that causes them. You should avoid the sun, too. And you must try lemon juice on your spots, Sal."

"Lordy, they'd never let me waste good lemons in such a worthless cause."

"Men do not deem beauty worthless, I think. As to the lemons, I shall waste them for you. Tell Cook I want a lemon a day for my complexion."

"With my old red hair, it don't hardly matter, milady."

"You will find the lemon also lightens your hair. It is not very red. I think it might tint to blond, if you use the lemons faithfully for a few months."

This sharing of wisdom and lemons was condescension of a high order, and it made Lady Helena a staunch friend.

"Mercy! You never mean it! No wonder the ladies are so jealous of their lemons. Can you use sugar, or must you take it straight?"

"*¿Qué?*" Helena blinked, then said as comprehension dawned, "You don't drink the juice. You put it on your face and hair."

"Well now!" Sally exclaimed in wonder.

"My navy pelisse, *por favor.*"

Lord Severn ran a practiced eye over his cousin when she descended the staircase. The dark bonnet and pelisse toned down any riotous Spanish excess to an acceptable level. He rather hoped the rain would let up, to allow him to show her off on Bond Street. They went out to the waiting carriage, arm in arm.

While the drizzle held up, Lady Helena was driven down Whitehall Street and shown the buildings where the wonders of British democracy were executed. They proceeded on foot to have a glance at the murky Thames, wandering idly by. It lacked the grandeur of the Guadalquivir at full flood. She was taken to see St. Paul's and peered through the thinning haze at its massive dome-topped bulk, which looked plain to her foreign eye, attuned to the flamboyance of Spanish baroque. Severn spoke at length of Christopher Wren and belabored the large dome.

"Papa has described it to me many times. I pictured something grander" was her comment. "Like the Santiago de Compostela, you know."

"Ah," Severn said, for he never liked to display his ignorance.

"It is the Cathedral of St. James of Compostela, in Santiago. He established Christianity in that area," she said vaguely. She was no authority on such things. "It is a marvelous old baroque church, with soaring steeples and very much ornate stonework. St. James was martyred in Jerusalem long ago, but his followers returned his body to Santiago. The wagon bearing his body was pulled by two wild bulls. The altar inside is a marvel of complexity," she announced grandly.

"Very interesting," he said in a bored voice.

"I listened to *your* speech on St. Paul's," she pointed out.

Severn disdained to reply to this childish outburst. He was happy to see she was bored. "Would you like to see where the Royal Family lives?"

"That would be most interesting!"

She found Buckingham Palace small, compared to the unending facade of the king of Spain's palace in Madrid, or the Escorial.

"We have a saying in English that comparisons are odious," he said haughtily, and next drove her past Carlton House. She could scarcely believe that the famous Prince Regent actually lived in that little hovel. "It is indescribably magnificent inside. And the gardens at the rear . . ."

She shrugged. "The Corinthian columns are well

enough, but not for a *prince*" was her indignant comment. "I have heard the Prince of Wales is a spendthrift, but I see the man is wronged. A prince living there! Why, it is not even clean. It needs a lick of whitewash."

"The prince will appreciate your sentiments, but pray do not express them to the taxpayers," he said. "Ah, I see a ray of sun is out. Let us go to Bond Street."

The sun burned away the layer of mist, and they descended to stroll along the fashionable shopping thoroughfare, where they encountered not less than three sets of bucks who ogled Helena. Although she appeared unconscious of the sensation she was causing, at last he had found something to please her. The bowfront windows held an array of items from around the world. She oohed over gewgaws and insisted on entering a shop featuring ladies' toys, where she expressed such interest in a red-and-gold silk fan with black slats that he bought it for her.

She lifted the fan and worked it with a flirtatious charm he had not seen before. It fluttered like a giant butterfly, now giving a glimpse of her dark eyes, now hiding them. He found these Spanish tricks enchanting but felt a strong inclination to limit their practice, like her mama's gowns, to Belgrave Square. Rutledge, he told himself, would not approve.

"It is all the crack, no?" she asked.

"Where the deuce did you pick up that expression? You have only been in London for less than a day. You must have learned it from the sailors aboard the *Princess Maria*."

"No, I heard it from Sally. And by the by, I must

33

have some lemons. One a day, for my complexion. I shall pay for them myself, of course, as I understand they are a delicacy in England. I must obtain some English money very soon. That can be easily done, *n'est-ce pas*? You see how quickly I am picking up the English idioms." She smiled. "Your mama is such a goose."

"It is not considered proper for a young lady to mock her elders," Severn said sternly.

"But I adore her! I meant no harm, truly," she said, her eyes large in chagrin.

"*Entre nous*, she *is* a bit of a goose," he allowed. She smiled in relief. It occurred to Severn that he ought to have been more severe, but with the sun shining and a pretty lady on his arm, he was in no mood for severity. "About your money—"

"I have a letter of credit from Papa's bank in Spain."

"I'll handle it for you this afternoon."

She lifted the fan, then slowly lowered it, revealing a soft smile. One gloved hand came out and touched his fingers. "What would I do without you, Eduardo?"

This wouldn't do! She was flirting with him, and he felt a pronounced desire to respond in kind. "I am happy to oblige you, Cousin," he said stiffly, and led her out the door.

"I may have to take you up on that offer."

"It will be my pleasure to serve you."

"Does pleasure always make you frown?" she teased.

"It is the sun in my eyes."

"That weak little candle! In Spain—but comparisons are odious."

"Just so," he said, relaxing into a smile.

Lady Helena's real interest was the ladies' toilettes, and here she was sadly disappointed when they resumed their walk. "Appalling!" she said, shaking her head in wonder. "Do the ladies have no figures to show off?"

"Indeed they do! And I wish you could convince them not to hide their figures. This is called the empress style, from France," he explained. He loathed it. It hung in a line from just below the bodice to the ankles, concealing everything between.

"I see that what English ladies consider elegant is what we wear to bed in Spain. It seems quite immodest to me to wear nightgowns in public, but if I must make myself ugly to accomplish a grand match, then I shall have some of these nightgowns made up immediately."

"When in Rome, you know," he said regretfully.

"Ah, but Rome did not wear such unflattering things as this. The men, too," she added, casting a glance on a brace of blue-jacketed bucks who strode by in the street. "They all dress alike. Is it a uniform, this inevitable blue jacket and fawn trousers? I notice you wear the same outfit, Eduardo."

"It is not a uniform! It is just what everyone wears."

"You would look so well in richer colors, a bordeaux jacket, or a deep green. But then you must avoid the vulgarity of being different, too, or you will not find a lady to marry you. You will require an *esposa* one day, I think?"

"You are speaking Spanish again," he reminded her, thus avoiding a reply to her question. A red or green jacket? He'd look a demmed jackanapes.

Though the colors would suit his dark hair and swarthy complexion . . .

She mentioned that she had brought one of her papa's jackets to use as a pattern for some new ones. Would Eduardo oblige her?

"Weston," he said. "I shall take it to him for you."

"Gracias." She turned to examine the ladies in the street. "What frightful coiffures," she said, conning the hairdos that peeped from below the bonnets. "They all have their hair hacked off like *muchachos'*."

"There is no need to cut your hair," he said. He admired her luxuriant sable hair. More than once, he had wondered how it would look set loose from its pins and cascading over her shoulders. It looked soft and smooth as silk.

"Oh, but I must be in fashion."

"Nonsense! You may set your own fashion in such details as coiffure."

"I sincerely wish I might set my own fashion in gowns, Eduardo. You don't think . . ."

With a memory of last night's emerald gown trimmed with black lace, he said, "I am afraid not, Helena. Perhaps after you are married; but the debs are scrutinized closely."

"I wonder how the gentlemen can be bothered to look at them," she said. "Shall we go into a drapery shop to look at the muslins?"

"I shall ask Mama to have a modiste bring samples with her. That will be easier for you," he replied.

Easier for him is what he means, she thought. But she was determined to conciliate him and smiled agreeably. "You are so thoughtful."

It was as they were driving home that Lady Helena said, "Do you happen to know a Mrs. Petrel-Jones, Eduardo?"

"I know of her," he replied, his lips tightening in a way she was coming to know denoted disapproval. "May I ask how you come to know a woman like that?"

"You mean lady, surely?" she asked, surprised.

"I am not so sure of that."

"Is there something amiss with her, then?"

"She is a widow, I believe, who has been jauntering about Europe. She showed up a year ago and managed to make a name for herself. How do you know her?"

"I met her in Spain. She was not a widow, but separated from her husband, who has died since then. She was received at Court," she added.

"Indeed! I cannot think the Spanish queen was very nice in her judgment." Not nearly so nice as Rutledge, who would think less of Helena if she took up with that rackety female.

"But your Prince of Wales does not live with his wife. In fact, from rumor, Princess Caroline is much worse than Mrs. Petrel-Jones."

"Oh, well, royalty may do as it pleases. I would not like you to seek out Mrs. Petrel-Jones. You are not likely to meet her anywhere that I take you. If she calls, we shall have Sugden tell her you are out. You shan't return her call, if she is so encroaching as to come running after you. Do you think it likely? Was she a close friend of yours in Spain?"

"Not a close friend. She is much older than I."

"Of course," he said, vastly relieved.

"She was a friend of Papa's."

"A pity Algernon's going to Spain."

37

Lady Helena was too astute to push her questions further at this time. She would soon find less exacting friends who would put her on to Mrs. Petrel-Jones. With a busy afternoon arranging for modistes and a coiffeur, and with a letter to write to Papa telling him that Mrs. Petrel-Jones was still single, she had no objection to returning to Belgrave Square.

Chapter Five

Over lunch, the ladies discussed modistes and gowns, and immediately after, Lady Hadley sent off a note to the Season's reigning queen of the needle, Madam Belanger. The bank note of a large denomination folded inside brought a prompt reply. Madam would attend her ladyship the next morning at eleven, with her samples and designs.

The afternoon's activities were delayed by a visit from Mrs. Audrey Comstock and her daughter Marion. Lady Helena's main interest was in the daughter, in whom she hoped to find a friend and confidante. Her hopes withered before Miss Comstock had uttered two sentences. Indeed they withered at the first glance of this "pale, unripened beauty of the north." Helena was convinced no lady who looked so very much like a Flemish painting could possibly have a thought in common with her.

It was unkindly said of Marion that her face was her chaperon. Her etiolated complexion looked as if she had spent the past month hiding under a rock. Her hair also had an unhealthy look and the consistency of dried grass. Her features—pale blue eyes, long nose, thin lips—wore that expression of strained tolerance often observed in Flemish portrayals of the Virgin.

"I am very happy to make your acquaintance, Cousin," Miss Comstock said. Her pale blue eyes raked Helena from head to toe. Marion was usually the first over the fence in pursuit of the Season's quarry, and she sensed stiff competition here.

"And I with you, Cousin," Helena replied stiffly. She wished to add some friendlier words, but those chilly eyes stopped her in her tracks.

"Lady Hadley tells me Severn showed you London this morning. It must have been exciting for you, after living in Spain." Her tone suggested that Spain might as well be Africa, so far as civilization went.

"Yes, indeed. It was quite . . . different."

For some obscure reason, Miss Comstock took this as a personal compliment and thanked her.

Mrs. Comstock, who was an older version of her daughter, with a layer of condescension added due to her age, said, "I have just been telling Lady Hadley we shall be happy to help her shoulder the burden of your debut, Lady Helena, for at her age, you know, it will be a sad imposition on her peace and quiet." Mrs. Comstock was a stripling of five and forty. "My Marion has already arranged her gowns and all that sort of thing. It will be a dreadful chore trying to find a modiste at this late hour. If I were not so busy, I would make some inquiries, but with the Season about to begin . . ."

"We have already arranged for Madam Belanger to come tomorrow morning, Audrey," Lady Hadley replied.

"That French creature? I daresay you had no choice, at so late a date. Odd your papa did not send you home sooner, Lady Helena."

"Spain is my home," Lady Helena said.

Next Mrs. Comstock turned her conversation to Lady Hadley. "You want to watch that Belanger. She is a Frenchie, you know. Her designs can be quite lascivious. Not suitable for a deb. I had Marion's gowns made up at Bath, before coming to London."

If the lifeless shroud encasing Marion's bones was an example of Bath couture, Helena was happy she had escaped such a fate.

Sherry and biscuits were served. Mrs. Comstock asked if it would be too much trouble to have tea for the youngsters. "I do not encourage Marion to take wine. It causes blotches. Indeed Lady Helena would be wise to avoid an excess of wine as well."

Determined to behave like a proper lady, Lady Helena drank the insipid liquid and conversed in stilted phrases with Miss Comstock for the half hour of the visit. When Mrs. Comstock rose, she repeated her offer to help shoulder the burden of Lady Helena's debut. The exact nature of her assistance was vague, except that she would call again soon to see how they were going on.

When the guests had left, Lady Helena asked in a small voice, "Are the Comstocks very good friends of yours, *Madrina*?"

"Audrey used to be, thirty-odd years ago. You will scarcely believe it, but when we made our bows together, she was one of the liveliest creatures you ever saw. Something has changed her. I don't know whether it was marrying an ecclesiastic or removing to Bath."

"Or having Marion for a daughter," Lady Helena added.

"Pour your cousin a glass of wine, Edward," Mrs. Comstock said. "She is going into a decline before our very eyes. I don't think we need worry too much about Audrey's assistance in 'shouldering the burden' of Helena's debut. I believe she came only out of curiosity, to get a look at her."

Lady Helena drew a great sigh of relief. "I am so glad you don't like them either," she said.

"Marion is not unattractive," Severn objected, but he knew he was lying. "There is no reason to disparage her. She is family, after all, and will be a suitable companion for Lady Helena. In behavior, she is all one could wish."

His mama rolled a jaundiced eye at him. "Don't let us detain you, Edward. Do you not have some business at the House? You were to see Brougham."

"I shall drop in for a few moments, at least. What will you ladies be up to this afternoon?"

"Lady Helena spoke of having a coiffeur in to tend to her hair. The ladies are wearing it shorter this year."

Severn scowled in displeasure. "I thought you disliked the do the ladies were sporting on Bond Street, Cousin. You mentioned their looking like moo—"

"Muchachos," she said. "Like little boys."

"You are to set your own style, I think? That boyish do would not suit you."

"Don't worry, Eduardo. I shall not disfigure myself. I shall need all the feminine allurements to nab a husband, shall I not, *Madrina*?"

Lady Hadley had gone off into a reverie, and when she spoke, it was on a different subject. *"Muchacho,* eh? There is another bit of Spanish for me. I think I can handle two new words a day. Tell me another."

"What word would you like to know, *Madrina*?"

"As you call me *Madrina*, why do I not call you by the Spanish for goddaughter? What would that be?"

"*Ahijada.*"

"God bless you. Not coming down with a cold, I hope?"

"But no. Why do you ask?"

"I think Helena means *ahijada* is Spanish for goddaughter?" he said, looking a question at her.

"Exactly."

"Good gracious, I could never get my tongue around that. Never mind, I shall call you Cousin-o instead. I know those Spaniards like to put an *o* at the ends of all their words."

A very confused Spanish lesson ensued. *Prima* led to so much confusion that in the end Helena agreed to the hybrid name *Cousina.*

"I can see something in the word displeases you, so I shall stick to plain old English," Severn said. "Good day, Cousin." He bowed and left.

Lady Hadley sent off for Alfredo, who was arranging all the better heads that Season. After much discussion and looking at sketches of coiffures, Lady Helena selected the *victime* do. "For my hair is naturally curly, and when it is short, it will curl by itself and remove the onus of using papers at night. I daresay Eduardo will not approve. He suggested I should keep my hair long."

"We shall not pay any attention to him," Lady Hadley said. "Now, where can we do the cutting without making a mess?"

She was not much inclined to leave her comfortable sofa. She had the servants lay papers on the floor and set a chair in the middle of the saloon for Helena. She watched as the sable locks fell from

43

the flying scissors. One flew beneath a side table and was left behind when Alfredo scooped up the rest. He knew a wig maker who would pay a fine penny for these specimens. Sally then washed Helena's hair, and Alfredo performed some magic with his brush until it sat in a cap of loose curls around her face.

"I feel light-headed," she exclaimed. "It will be such a relief not to have all that hair pinned up. The pins quite give me the megrims after a long day. Do you like it, *Madrina*?"

"I feared the *victime* would look dowdy," she said, "for it was all the crack twenty or more years ago. It was named for the victims of the revolution in France, you must know. I don't know exactly why, for it was the heads they cut off, not the hair, but so it is. However, it does not look in the least dowdy. Folks do say that if you hold on to old things long enough, they will come back into style. I wonder if I could get away with that bonnet I bought in eighteen hundred."

"Perhaps with that hairdo, you could, your ladyship," Alfredo said daringly.

"Why, thank you, Alfredo." She smiled and bid him adieu.

"That was a very pretty compliment, was it not, *Cousina*?" she said when they were alone. "But I put no faith in the compliments of coiffeurs or modistes. It is all part and parcel of their trade. Well, it is time to change for dinner. I wonder if Edward will be back. His papa would often stay at the House till late into the night, scheming with his cohorts. Their meetings had something to do with unseating the Tories," she confided with a sage nod. "Now that I have talked Edward into calling on Brougham, I daresay he will always be busy, too. Brougham is the leader of the Whigs."

Lady Helena knew that keeping Severn in good curl was important to her comfort, and she made a careful toilette for dinner. As they were dining at home, she felt free to wear one of her late mama's more dashing gowns. It was a rich peacock blue, drawn tightly at the waist and flaring below. The top was cut low but not immodestly so. She pinned a white silk rose into her curls.

Over her shoulder she said to Sally, "I asked *Madrina* to send up a lemon each day. Did Cook give it to you, Sally?"

"Yes, miss, I've already squeezed one, but the freckles are still with me."

"It takes a little while." She took a last look in the mirror. "Do I look all right?"

"You look like a queen, miss. The Spanish queen," she added, as it struck her that Queen Charlotte could not touch Lady Helena for looks.

Lady Helena made a moue. "If you knew Queen Maria Luisa, you would realize that is not a compliment."

"Ain't she pretty, then?"

"She has a face like a hatchet."

"You have to wonder how she ever nabbed a king. I daresay it's like you and Lord Severn—an arranged match, for the money and all." Helena looked at her strangely. "I shouldn't be gossiping, milady. It's only what Lord Severn's valet said, that Lord Hadley told his son he'd best marry you, if he knew what was good for him."

"Of course," Helena said, and dismissed her servant. So Lord Severn was under orders, was he? No wonder he was chafing at the bit. If his aim was to

45

marry her, he was surely setting about it in an odd way. One could hardly describe his behavior as gallant. Yet he was not behaving badly enough to give a lady a total disgust of him, if his aim was to win a refusal. He was lukewarm, lacking the courage to flout his papa and hoping his indifference would make her reject him. A coward, in other words. Her lip curled in disdain. But until she had devised her strategy, she would continue to be pleasant.

Belowstairs, Lord Severn had been notified that Lady Helena had had the coiffeur in during his absence. "Yes, Edward, she had all her hair chopped off, and I must say it looks lovely," his mother informed him.

"What! I told her not to!"

"My dear, that is hardly your place! I am her chaperon, and I agreed to it. The poor child's head aches from carrying such a load of pins to loop her curls up. You men have no idea what we have to put up with to make ourselves presentable. Strawberry packs to bleach our skin, and having our hair cranked up in papers and never allowed to go out in the sun. Lessons in walking and talking and dancing and pouring tea. We might as well be racehorses, for all we do is train, train, train, until we nab a *parti*. And *then* we are expected to bear children. Do you think that is a picnic? I think we must all be saints without knowing it."

Severn's real wrath was not with his mama, but with Lady Helena. He had asked her not to cut her hair. That she had done so showed a disregard for his opinion that not only annoyed but greatly surprised him. Her behavior until now had suggested that she admired and liked him.

He was ready to be as stiff as starch when she

appeared belowstairs in her new coiffure. He would not denigrate it. He would be more subtle than that. "Very nice," he would say with a pained look that revealed his true opinion. All those lovely curls gone forever . . .

But when she appeared without warning at the doorway of the saloon, the breath caught in his throat. She looked like a vision out of some exotic Eastern tale. Her mama's peacock gown hugged the contours of her lithe body. Above it, an unseemly expanse of creamy flesh rose enticingly. The hair, much as it vexed him to admit it, looked charming. A black riot of curls bounced when she walked forward and made an exquisite curtsy.

"I, in case you don't recognize me, am your cousin Helena, Eduardo," she said, with an arch smile. "Please don't say I look horrid! The deed is done now, and I am stuck with it. What do you think?"

"Very nice," he said, in not quite the strained voice he had prepared.

She turned a saucy smile on her godmama. "There, *Madrina*! I told you he would like it. Gentlemen never know what they like until they are shown."

"Gentlemen have entirely too much to say about what they like, if you want *my* opinion," Lady Hadley said, with an angry glare at her son. "They do not ask us if we like *their* hair all hacked off like those moochachies in Spain. They are too wise to be bothered doing their hair up in papers for *us*. Why should *we* carry the burden of having to be ornaments, I should like to know?" Having delivered this piece of spleen, she added, "You look very nice, dear, and never mind what he says. Get *Cou-*

sina a glass of wine, Edward. One would think you were bred in a stable.''

While they enjoyed their wine, Severn pestered them with some very dull *on-dits* from Westminster. He had agreed to act as temporary chancellor of the exchequer in the shadow cabinet until a permanent appointment was made. He feared it was a horrible mistake. He had no idea how much money the Tories were squandering or how much work was involved preparing questions to raise in the House. A large case of papers awaited him in his study, but it would all stand him in good stead with his father later.

Lady Hadley had the inspiration of discussing *Cousina*'s ball to stop the flow of financial talk, and this filled the remainder of the meal more interestingly.

Severn took his port alone and was astonished to see, when he went to join the ladies, that Helena had retired to her room to write some letters and peruse the latest fashion magazines.

"Did you tell her I was going out?" he asked his mama.

"No, dear, I most particularly told her you were remaining at home this evening. Perhaps that is why she decided to go abovestairs. I believe I shall do the same."

On this set-down, she rose and left Severn alone, staring at the walls and wondering where he had gone wrong. Helena, while all smiles and charm when he was present, obviously cared nothing for him. A few questions from his bachelor friends at the House had alerted him that Helena was likely to cause quite a stir when she was let loose in society. "Who was that Incomparable you were on the strut with this morning, Severn?" one had asked. Several had asked permission to call and be presented to Lady Helena.

He rose and began pacing. Something at the edge of a side table caught his eye, and he bent over to pick it up. It was a lock of sable hair. *Her* hair, soft and silky. He looked about in vain for somewhere to dispose of it. The side table had a drawer. He drew it open and dropped the curl in on top of a few newspaper clippings yellowing with age. Then he went like a lamb to the slaughter to peruse the large volume of papers awaiting him in his study.

Chapter Six

Life was a busy whirl of preparations over the next fortnight. The first priority was to have some suitable gowns made up for Lady Helena to wear even before the formal commencement of the Season. The obliging Madam Belanger worked her minions overtime so that her ladyship might make a decent appearance when she received company at home and when she enjoyed such informal outings as tea parties and drives. There were also Lady Helena's presentation at court and her own ball to arrange. Due to her late arrival, her ball would not occur until the middle of May. Even in advance of her presentation to the queen, she enjoyed a raft of callers. As circumstances permitted, she made discreet inquiries for Mrs. Petrel-Jones, but she had no luck in finding anyone who knew her.

Lady Hadley could only wonder at her son's smiles when *Cousina* was such a great success. Did he not realize every caller was a rival? He seemed to be spending more and more time at Whitehall. Mrs. Comstock and her daughter's calls became a daily event, once they discovered where all the gentlemen were hiding themselves. Their condescension did not diminish with familiarity. Quite the contrary, even Miss Comstock took to dropping Lady Helena hints as to her conduct.

"You must not be too familiar with gentlemen, Cousin," she cautioned, "or they might try to take advantage of you." Her sharp look seemed to suggest she had suffered this fate, which was so ridiculous that Helena completely ignored her advice.

The ball and the presentation gown were very expensive. When Lady Hadley complained that she could not keep track of so many bills and checks, Severn, now the financial wizard of the family, volunteered to take charge of the banking. He deemed it prudent to read Lady Helena a lecture when he got the bill for her presentation gown.

"You must bear in mind that this gown is not likely to be worn again. It is too ornate for an ordinary ball."

"But I must look well to make my curtsy to the queen."

"Certainly you want to make a good impression. I think a good impression might have been made in a gown that cost less than three hundred and fifty pounds, however. I seem to recall Marion's cost a third of that when she was presented."

"I shall bear it in mind, Eduardo," she said. But her mischievous smile hardly denoted obedience to his hint. "We shall see whether it was worth it when the time comes."

"Meaning what?"

"Why, which of us makes the better match. You have not forgotten Papa expects me to make a great match?"

"Then you will not be choosing your husband from the crew who litter the saloon every afternoon." Rutledge, though interested in sherry, had proved elusive.

"Oh, no, they are only for practice." She smiled. "And you need not disparage them, for they were not invited by me. They are your friends from the House."

Left with no rebuttal, he scoffed, "Tories, half of them."

"As the Tories are in power and have been for years, the great men of England must be Tories," she pointed out.

"You will find few great men on the right side of the House."

"How could they be on the wrong side?" she asked, perplexed, and received a lecture on the seating that prevailed in Parliament.

Severn enjoyed these tête-à-têtes, during which he could instruct Helena in those areas where his own expertise, such as it was, was at least greater than hers. He enjoyed her company and could indulge himself without verging into the dangerous territory of romance. She always listened closely and displayed more interest than she did, in fact, feel. She knew this master-pupil arrangement pleased a gentleman.

After one of his lessons, Severn was always willing to do as she wished. That particular lesson induced him to purchase a tilbury for her. When she mentioned that Mr. Wetherby, one of her drawing-room conquests, had offered to teach her to drive, it also induced him to give her driving lessons himself.

"Let that cow-handed fellow teach you to drive? He has no more notion of driving than a dog has of flying."

"Sutherland, I believe, is a noted fiddler," she suggested. "He also mentioned he would be willing—"

"Willing to drive you to Gretna Green and marry your fortune. There is nothing else for it; I must teach you myself."

Helena was indifferent as to who taught her, so long as she learned to drive. "You are too kind, Eduardo," she said.

For a week they had a lesson each day, beginning on the sparsely traveled roads of the countryside and eventually venturing into town when she had achieved some competence. And for the whole week, they enjoyed each other's company with a very minimum of bickering. Helena admired Severn's skillful handling of the ribbons. He never led her into dangerous situations, but, on the other hand, he did not hold her back by undue caution either. Severn was also impressed with her courage and judgment.

"Do you feel up to passing that rig ahead of us?" he asked. "It cannot be going more than five miles an hour. Such a sluggardly pace takes the pleasure out of driving."

"The road is not very wide," she said, gauging her space.

"Lead your team as far as possible to the side. He'll move over when he hears you behind him. This is a good, straight stretch of road to try it. No one is coming. Ready?"

Her pulse raced with the thrill of giving the team their head. The other carriage moved over, just as he had said, and she squeaked past. "Well done!" Severn congratulated.

At the end of the week, she had mastered city

traffic and felt capable of dispensing with Severn's assistance.

She couched her dismissal slyly. "I feel very bad, keeping you from the important business of the House, Eduardo," she said as they had a glass of wine after their drive. "It was kind of you to give me so much of your time, but I must not be selfish. Now I know how to drive, and you need not waste your valuable time driving out with me."

Severn felt a strange reluctance to see the drives stop. "It will not be proper for you to drive about town alone."

"*Madrina* says that as long as I have a groom with me, there will be no impropriety."

"A groom is all well and good, but it would be best if you had a proper escort."

"That is no problem. Wetherby would like to be taken aboard, and Lord John Simcoe has also offered—"

"Those rackety fellows! They are worse than no one. Wetherby's idea of driving is hunting the squirrel. He ran Lord Mansbridge off the highway only last week."

"And yet I cannot prevail further on your kindness. I am sure Brougham must need you at the House."

Brougham was indeed questioning his frequent absences, but that was not what impelled Severn to drop in so often. He found, almost to his dismay, that he enjoyed the work and was good at it. His sharp eye was quick to pick out discrepancies in the figures issued by the government. He had gotten Vansittart on the hot seat the day before and given him a good roasting. Papa would be proud of him.

"Perhaps you are right. I have been shirking my

parliamentary duties. A groom will do well enough as your escort, but not Misener, mind! He is too lackadaisical. Use Foster."

"Whatever you think best, Eduardo," she agreed. Foster would be easily managed. The older men were often more biddable than the younger.

Severn left, having acquiesced to her plan and feeling he was becoming quite a dab at handling his cousin.

The next day before the Comstocks arrived, Helena set out for Bond Street. Moira, Mrs. Petrel-Jones, greatly enjoyed shopping. Lady Helena thought Bond Street the likeliest place to find her. As driving was still new to her, it took most of her attention. She did not see Mrs. Petrel-Jones, but Marion Comstock and her mama saw Helena and were in the saloon at Belgrave Square early the next day. Marion was properly bonneted for driving in the open carriage.

"We felt sorry for you yesterday, having to drive all alone, Cousin," Marion said. "It looked so very odd, you must know. Mama has told me I must accompany you from thenceforth."

"How kind," Lady Helena said in a dying voice.

She knew she must advance her drives to the morning, but for that afternoon she was burdened with Cousin Marion. Before long, the Argus-eyed Marion noticed that Helena was paying more attention to the pedestrians than to her driving. Odder still, it seemed to be the ladies she was ogling, despite her vulgar interest in gentlemen at all other times.

"Are you looking for someone, Cousin?" she asked.

"No!" Helena said. For some unaccountable reason, her eyes flew to her reticule, resting on the seat between them.

It was hanging open—such carelessness was typical of Helena. She took no heed of her belongings. She had complained of losing a glove and a silk scarf during previous shopping expeditions. As Helena was fully occupied with her driving, Marion took a peek into the reticule. A letter was wedged in between her money purse and a hairbrush. A billet-doux?

When Helena drew to a halt a little later to exchange greetings with Mr. Wetherby, Marion slid the letter out. It was not addressed to Helena, yet its well-worn appearance suggested it had been in her possession for some time. The name on the envelope was Moira, with no last name, which looked like a letter to be delivered by hand. The opening had come loose. Marion unfolded the corner and took a peek. It was all in Spanish. How very odd! Helena had not mentioned having a Spanish friend in town. Why did she make a secret of it? There was bound to be something underhanded in it. Perhaps Severn would know. She quickly slid the letter back into the reticule and jiggled Helena's arm. "You are holding up traffic, Cousin."

Helena looked behind her and saw a rig approaching a block away. No one was waiting to proceed.

"May I call this evening?" Mr. Wetherby asked.

"Certainly not!" Helena replied flirtatiously. "We are being presented tomorrow and attending our first ball in the evening. Such grand ventures require hours of beatifying. But I shall save you a dance at Lady Perth's ball tomorrow night."

"The first one?"

"Best make it the second. Sorry, but I really should give Severn the first, I expect."

"The second, then. *A demain.*"

Wetherby lifted his hat and continued on his way.

Miss Comstock's nose was put out of joint by Helena's casual mention of having the first dance with Severn. She had been planning to give him that honor herself. Yet she was not entirely disconsolate. Clearly Severn had not asked her. "I really should give Severn the first" was what she had said. They would see about that.

Meanwhile, her mind continued to play with the name Moira. It was not a common name, like Elizabeth or Jane. She knew only one Moira. There was a Miss Moira FitzGerald making her curtsy that spring. By a circuitous route, she led the conversation to their debut, mentioning various ladies. "And of course Moira FitzGerald," she said. "Do you know her, Cousin?"

"No, I don't know any of the girls. How should I? Is she a particular friend of yours?"

"Not particularly. Let us get off busy Bond Street, Cousin. The park would be less strenuous driving for you."

It was nearly four, the hour at which the fashionable set met at the barrier at Hyde Park. Helena drove there. She met several friends but caught not a glimpse of Mrs. Petrel-Jones.

From Hyde Park they drove directly to Belgrave Square, where Mrs. Comstock was awaiting Marion's return. Severn had come back early from the House. He had left as soon as he noticed that Wetherby was not in his usual seat.

"You have been gone for hours," Mrs. Comstock

exclaimed. "I feared Cousin Helena had dumped you in the ditch."

"Why, ma'am," Helena said, "you hurt my feelings to say so. I am becoming a notable whip, am I not, Marion?"

"Cousin Helena managed to keep out of the ditches," Marion allowed. "We talked to Mr. Wetherby, then drove to the park."

"Wetherby ought to have been in the House," Severn said severely. "We were discussing measures to pay for the war."

Mrs. Comstock said, "Have your tea, Marion, then we must be going."

Helena poured herself a glass of wine and joined the older ladies. Marion took her teacup and sat beside Severn. "I fear you are in Wetherby's bad books, Severn," she said.

"He is in mine, missing an important meeting. He is supposed to be Lord Ward's secretary. Why do you say—"

"Lady Helena wanted to have the first dance with him at Lady Perth's ball tomorrow. She was very sorry that she feels obliged to stand up first with you."

"I have not asked her for the first dance," he said at once. "Though as her host, I daresay it is to be expected." It rankled, though, that she did it reluctantly.

"As she and Wetherby are such particular friends, perhaps you should give him precedence."

"What do you mean? His constant harassment of Helena hardly qualifies him for special treatment. Demmed jackanapes."

"It was just an idea," she said. "Lady Helena dislikes being bound by the proprieties. That unfortunate tendency to loose behavior is due entirely to her upbringing, for I feel she is basically a good-natured creature. She moved her carriage along as soon as I pointed out that she and Wetherby were holding up traffic in the middle of Bond Street."

"It is well you were there. I feared some such disaster if she were out alone."

"Perhaps I am making too much of it. It was all Wetherby's fault. He rattles on so." She noticed that the name of Wetherby incited Severn to a fit of jealousy and was clever enough to realize that another suitor only enhanced Helena in his eyes.

"I cannot think her affections are seriously engaged, for she refused to let him call this evening. Being warned off from him will only make him appear more attractive. It would be best to let them have their opening dance together."

"No one is stopping her, if that is what she wishes."

"There is her sense of duty to you, Severn. If you just mention that your first dance is taken—"

"But she is my cousin, staying here with Mama."

"I am also your cousin. I'll give you the first dance. Would that serve the purpose?" She sat, awaiting his decision.

Caught in the middle of irritation with Helena—that "sense of duty" smote his ear harshly—and Wetherby and himself, and gratitude to Marion for her word of warning, he said, "Very kind of you, Marion. Will you do me the honor of giving me the opening minuet?"

"With pleasure," she said, and set down her cup. "I should be leaving. Oh, by the way, Severn, did you ever hear Helena mention someone called Moira?"

"I cannot recall. Why do you ask?"

"Just curious. The name came up in conversation, but I didn't think to follow it up. She was driving so recklessly! I rather think this Moira was someone she met in Spain. No matter. I wish you will not say I mentioned it, for I had an idea she did not wish to discuss it." She rose and went to her mother, and soon they left.

"I thought they would never leave," Lady Hadley said. "It is time to dress for dinner. Your gown for Lady Perth's ball arrived, *Cousina*. It is in your room."

When Lady Hadley went upstairs, Severn remained behind. "I hear you met Wetherby during your drive," he said to Helena.

"We had a few words on Bond Street."

"I daresay he was pestering you for the first dance?"

"He was, but I put him off. I saved the first dance for you, Eduardo, in repayment for all your kindness."

"That was not necessary, I assure you," he said, disliking that touch of condescension.

"Oh, but I wanted to!"

He felt a surge of frustration. "Actually, I have engaged to stand up with Marion for the first set," he said stiffly.

Helena's full lips drew into a moue without her even realizing it. "I see." She was considerably surprised to discover that she was angry. She had thought she had Severn firmly enamored of her and thus ready to do her bidding. A Severn led by Marion was another thing entirely.

Severn observed her pique and was heartened. Marion was right, by God! "Shall we say the second dance?" he asked.

She flounced her shoulders. "Perhaps. We shall see. And now I must change for dinner."

Chapter Seven

The presentation to the queen was a grand affair, with all the young ladies on their best behavior. Lady Helena observed that England was burdened with an even uglier queen than Spain was, and one not nearly so finely rigged out. The presentation was mere pomp and ritual. The real opening of the Season occurred that evening at a much livelier do, Lady Perth's ball.

"I look *fea!*" Lady Helena exclaimed, studying herself in the mirror before going belowstairs. "It is this cursed white gown, of all colors the most bland."

"You look lovely, milady," Sally assured her. "Which of your corsages will you wear? Four sets of flowers, and you've never shown your face at a real ball yet. Lord John's pink roses would give you a touch of color."

"I shall wear Lord Severn's orchid," she said, and pinned it into place. It still rankled that he had refused the first dance with her. Was it possible that he and Marion were in love? She saw none of the usual symptoms, yet he had asked Marion to be his first partner, when his papa had ordered him to offer for herself. Perhaps he was merely flexing his independence. . . .

She pinched her cheeks and bit her lips to a rosy hue before descending the staircase. She fully expected Severn would be awaiting her at the foot of the stairs, as he often was. He was not there, and her ire rose a notch. But when she entered the saloon and he came to meet her, she was put back in humor by the admiration gleaming in his eyes.

"You look—*bella*, Cousin," he said. His dark eyes flickered to the orchid, and a smile of satisfaction grew.

She performed an exquisite curtsy, bowing low, as she had done that afternoon to the queen.

"Do get up, *Cousina*. It hurts my legs to see you all crouched over," Lady Hadley said. "You do us proud. Very *bella*. When did *you* learn a word of Spanish, Edward?"

Lady Hadley was accompanying them on this first do of the Season and was rigged out for the occasion in a violet gown, with a clutch of feathers in her coiffure.

"That word, I believe, is international," Severn replied.

"It applies equally to you, *Madrina*," Helena said. "Very elegant! You will take the shine out of all the matrons."

"I am long past trying for anything of the sort," Lady Hadley lied, and patted her curls complacently.

Helena said, "It remains only to assure Eduardo that he, too, looks *muy bello*, and we are ready to leave."

"Oh, ho!" Lady Severn exclaimed. "You see what *Cousina* thinks of your toilette, Edward. She is calling you one of those moochachies."

"Indeed, no! Milord looks very mature and sober in his black jacket."

Severn assumed this was meant as a compliment, but he found little pleasure in looking mature and sober when he was accustomed to being called dashing and handsome.

"The carriage is waiting. Shall we go?" he said.

The ladies got their cloaks and they were off, lumbering through streets busy with traffic now that the Season had officially begun. Smaller routs were in progress at some of the houses, with carriages lined up and members of the ton, all decked out in their finery, alighting. The greatest congestion was at Lady Perth's mansion on Grosvenor Square, where the carriages were lined up for a block. The impatient young folks in some of the carriages alighted and walked to the door.

Helena knew just how they felt. She, too, wanted to alight and dash to the doorway. She was eager to pitch herself into this new life. Perhaps this was the evening she would meet her husband-to-be. She envisaged a gallant in the Spanish style, with dangerously flashing eyes and a reckless smile. He would be wearing a jacket of bordeaux, with a fall of white lace at the throat and sleeves. Before the night was over, he would proclaim his love for her.

But, of course, they waited until they were near the door before alighting, because of Lady Hadley. When they stood on the landing to be announced, Helena scanned the floor below for her lover-to-be and saw not a single bordeaux jacket. All the gentlemen had been hounded into plain black evening suits by Beau Brummell. At least two-thirds of them appeared to have blond hair and pale skin.

She caused enough stir to flatter her vanity, however, and went below with some interest. Marion appeared like a wraith to claim her partner. This left Helena unpartnered, but not for long. Several of her courtiers advanced to welcome her. She gave the first dance to Wetherby, as she sensed this might annoy Severn—she wished, for some unfathomable reason, to annoy him. He looked pleased with himself as he led Marion to the floor.

They did not share a set, and as the dance proceeded, Helena kept an eye on her cousins. She reluctantly admitted that they made a regal-looking couple, both tall and elegant. She noticed that the other ladies in her set were watching them as well. Clearly it was not Marion who had caught their eye. It seemed Eduardo was considered a desirable *parti*.

When the dance was finished, one of the ladies in her set, Miss McIntosh, said, "You are Severn's cousin. Will you present me to him for the next set? He is very handsome, is he not?"

"I am promised to Severn for the next set," she said.

"Introduce me, then. I'll nab him for another dance."

Helena made the introduction, but she did it reluctantly. Miss McIntosh, a Scottish heiress, was very pretty and was considered one of the Season's Incomparables. Helena's dance with Severn was a cotillion, and while he was perfectly polite, he was not gallant. He did not tell her she was the prettiest girl at the ball or admire her considerable skill in dancing.

What he said was, "I have been scouting out a couple of England's great men for you, Cousin. I shall present you to the Duke of Rutledge at the end of this set."

"Which one is he?" she asked.

"The fellow in the set just to the left of us, the tall one with blond hair."

She glanced and saw what she was coming to consider a typical Englishman. Tall, blond, pale, blue eyes, with a long nose and no charm.

"He is a duke, you say?"

"A very eligible duke."

"Aren't any of the dukes handsome?"

"No. For some reason, beauty and money seldom go hand in hand in England."

She scanned other gentlemen and soon found one whose appearance interested her. He was a little older than the other bachelors, but with a reckless air about him that appealed to her. "Who is the black-haired fellow with Miss Perkins?" she inquired.

Severn looked around until he found him. "Not one of our great men. He is a here-and-thereian, of good breeding, but not a feather to fly with. No doubt he will nab some heiress from the provinces, but you, I think, may look higher."

"But what is his name, Eduardo?"

"Malvern. Allan Malvern, I believe. Some connection to the Beauforts. You will not want to waste your time on him."

The next set saw Severn standing up with Miss McIntosh, and Helena with the Duke of Rutledge.

"I hear you have recently arrived from Spain," the duke said. She admitted it and was subjected to an intelligent discussion of sherry.

There was some air of condescension in him that she did not like. His haughty mien suggested he was doing her a favor to stand up with her. He was mature and intelligent, but utterly lacking in romance. One would think he might spare at least a moment for a compliment.

"Are you always so serious at a ball, Your Grace?" she asked when he ran out of questions.

The duke had made his assessment. Lady Helena had passed his high standard of acceptability. "What a fool you must think me! Here I am dancing with the prettiest lady at the ball, and I inundate her with talk of grape cultivation, which you must be tired of hearing. It is not often that I meet anyone who has actually lived at Jerez. They say it is a combination of the soil and the grape found there that gives your sherry its unique taste."

"That is usually the way with all great wines."

He shook his head ruefully. "Oh, Lord, I am discussing wine again. I shall do better tomorrow—if you will allow me to call?"

"I will be honored, Your Grace."

Helena always kept at the back of her mind that she must find Mrs. Petrel-Jones. She did not expect to find her at such a prestigious do as Lady Perth's ball, nor did she. She also felt it unlikely that the duke would know her and did not ask him. Who seemed a likelier person was Mr. Malvern. He was a little older and had the dashing look of Moira's friends.

Meeting him proved difficult. Severn kept her supplied with a series of staid aristocratic bachelors. After dinner, when a set of waltzes was announced, she slipped away to the card room to see how *Madrina* was going on, and there she met Malvern. The debs were not allowed to waltz until the patronesses of Almack's gave their permission.

The meeting was not quite by chance, but the arranging was contrived by Malvern, who had noticed her noticing him. He was waiting just beyond the room when she left and stepped forth to jostle her, as if by accident.

"I'm terribly sorry! So clumsy of me!" he said, steadying her with a hand on her arm. Then he looked into her eyes and smiled a dashing smile of the sort not often seen in England. "And of course my gaucherie has to be perpetrated on the loveliest lady in London. The Fates dislike me, I swear." His hand lingered on her arm a moment before he removed it.

He towered a good six inches over her. His jacket, black, to be sure, but of the finest cut, clung like the skin on a peach to his broad, straight shoulders. His hair was jet black and shining. She could not find a single flaw on his face, except perhaps for a trace of art in his smile.

"I daresay it is pointless for me to hope for a dance, now that you have discovered my two left feet?"

"I seldom dance with strangers, sir," she replied, but in no daunting way.

"That is easily remedied. I have a name here somewhere, but your beauty has put it quite out of my mind. Ah yes, now I have it—Mal something. A bad omen, you are thinking—*mal* being French for 'bad.' Ah, now I have it! Malvern. That is plain Mr. Malvern. No proud noble lineage, but one of my names goes back to the year one. I was christened Peter Allan, as in Saint Peter. I do not claim a blood kinship with any saint, however. Folks soon took my measure and called me Allan."

"What a lot of nonsense you talk. I did not mistake you for one of the Apostles, Mr. Malvern."

"No, I am old, but not quite that old. I do fear my hearing might be going, though. I did not hear your name. No matter, the whole of London knows by now that you are Lady Helena Carlisle, that you escaped Spain in a wheelbarrow of cabbages—no, I am mistaking you for one of the French refugees. In any case, I know you are Severn's cousin, and he is keeping you mighty close. I have also seen for myself that you are a fine Terpsichore. Dare I hope . . . ?"

"I would be happy to dance with you, Mr. Malvern, but I fear the next set is to be waltzes. That is why I paid a visit to the card room at this time."

"You dislike them that much, do you? Pity. I am fond of them myself. It is the only time I get my arms around a lady. But I would sacrifice anything, even my beloved waltz, for a further opportunity to pester you with my nonsense. May I get you a glass of wine?"

"Thank you. I would like one. Nonsense always makes me thirsty for wine."

"That is odd. I find it just the other way around. Wine turns me nonsensical."

"Then I don't think you need any more."

"Oh, I adore being nonsensical. It is not as easy as folks think."

He led her to the refreshment parlor to procure wine; then they returned to the ballroom to watch the waltzers.

"I wonder, Mr. Malvern, do you happen to know a Mrs. Petrel-Jones?" she asked. "I knew her in Spain. She has returned to London, but I have not been able to discover her."

Malvern had never heard of her, but he was eager to continue the acquaintance with Lady Helena and indulged in a little prevarication. "I recognize the name. I recall the lady had come from Spain, but I'm afraid I don't know her well. You might put an advertisement in the journals. If she doesn't see it, someone is bound to tell her."

"Oh, I couldn't do that!" she exclaimed without thinking. Malvern looked surprised. "She would have to get in touch with me at Lord Severn's place, and I fear he would not approve. Not that there is anything wrong with her!"

"Not lofty enough to be a friend of Lady Helena's?"

"He feels she flies too high for a younger lady like me."

"Yes, she is a trifle below your touch. I wonder why you wish to renew the acquaintance?"

"Because I like her. And I have a letter for her from a mutual friend in Spain. If you happen to see her—"

"I'll do better than that. I shall seek her out and let you know when I find her. Will it be permissible for me to call on you, or shall we have a clandestine correspondence?"

"Of course you may come," she said at once. Severn had said Malvern's family was good, and, after all, she did not plan to make him a bosom bow. "I would appreciate it very much if you could find her."

"I shall make it my first priority, milady. Expect me very soon. And now if you will excuse me, I have promised the next set to Mrs. Morgan." He bowed and took his leave.

When he left, Helena looked at the waltzers. She saw Severn staring icily at her over the shoulder of a blond lady. He had seen her with Malvern, but no matter. She would explain that they had literally bumped into each other. No harm in that. Severn looked away after one fierce glare, but Helena kept watching him as he twirled gracefully around the floor. She didn't recognize the pretty blonde, but she observed that Severn seemed quite interested in her. That smile did not denote a discussion of politics, but of flirtation.

As soon as the waltzes were finished, he returned the blonde to her chaperon and joined Helena. "I see you managed to scrape an acquaintance with Malvern," he said, in a tight-lipped way that always got her back up.

She decided not to explain. "Yes, he is quite charming."

He drew out his watch and said, "Good Lord! Look at the time. Mama will be exhausted. We really should get her home."

"I did not plan to dance with Mr. Malvern, Eduardo," she said with a knowing look. "But if you are tired, by all means, let us leave."

"Perhaps a word with Rutledge before going."

"Not necessary. He is calling on me tomorrow."

"You don't waste any time!"

"Neither does he," she riposted, peering to see how Severn reacted. A satisfied smile settled on his lips.

Before long, Helena had figured out his strategy. If she accepted an offer from the duke, then Severn would not have to marry her. He was off the hook. "Actually, he is a dead bore," she said, "but one cannot like to refuse a duke permission to call."

"Oh, a great man, Rutledge. A great man."

Chapter Eight

"Well, my dear, and how did you enjoy meeting the great men of England?" Lady Hadley inquired the next morning over breakfast.

"I do not believe I met any, *Madrina*," Lady Helena replied, with a quizzing look at Severn.

Lady Hadley said, "Now there you are mistaken, *Cousina*, for though he looks like a schoolmaster at the end of term, all pale and worn, young Rutledge is the greatest *parti* to be had. A duke! How could you hope to do better? You would not want any of the royal princes, I assure you. They are a sorry lot. Rutledge is very well to grass. He owns vast acres—and in Kent and Hampshire, too, close to London, not in some of those godforsaken countries in the north, like your papa's."

"I do not care for a title or wealth, *Madrina*," Lady Helena said indignantly. Lady Hadley and her son stared in confusion. "When I refer to a great man, I mean a man of great affairs in the nation. A member of the cabinet, or a famous man in science or the arts. And, of course, I should prefer that he be young and somewhat dashing. The foolish English side of me is attracted by appearances, I admit."

"Oh, my dear *Cousina*," Lady Hadley said, "we

71

English are never foolish, I assure you, not about making matches. I wager the Spanish mamas don't hold a candle to us when it comes to finding a good *parti* for our gels." She glanced at Severn and added, "And our sons, come to that."

"You will find very few of England's great men are young," Severn informed her. "Until a gentleman is thirty, he is called 'promising.' Only at a more mature age are great affairs entrusted to him."

Helena said, "Yet your Mr. Pitt was prime minister at twenty-four, and Byron, at an even younger age, achieved greatness as a poet. I call that more than promising."

"There are exceptions to every rule," he said vaguely.

"Then perhaps what I require is not a great man, but an exceptional one. Do you know any such gentlemen, Eduardo?"

"I do not, and if I did, it is just possible, you know, that they would hope to marry an exceptional lady."

Lady Helena's eyes narrowed dangerously. "One does not hear of Lord Byron looking so high, I believe?"

"One doesn't hear of him marrying any of his flirts either."

"Mostly because they are all married already," Lady Hadley pointed out. "And in some cases divorced, and married again. You do not want to have anything to do with Byron, my dear. He has the looks and dash you mentioned liking, but one is beginning to hear some shady things about that fellow."

"Actually, Papa does not expect me to marry a prime minister or anything like that. When I speak of a great man, I mean only someone who is involved in the serious affairs of the country. Someone like you, Eduardo." He looked at her musingly, while a slow smile crept across his lips. "Only, of course, younger and . . . more . . . younger," she repeated. Her lashes quivered as if in embarrassment.

"Why, Edward is only thirty," his mama exclaimed.

Helena blinked in surprise. "Really? I thought you must be closer to forty, Eduardo." That would teach him to try to palm her off on boring Rutledge.

"You are mistaken," he said in a chilly voice. "And now, though only a small cog in the affairs of Parliament, I must go and attend to business. Good day, ladies."

After he had left, Lady Helena gave a little grimace. "Have I hurt his feelings, *Madrina*?"

"I shouldn't worry about it, my dear. Perhaps you have given his pride a little blow, but that never does a fellow any harm. So you are seeing Rutledge today? A pity you could not care for him. A dash of hot Spanish blood is just what that family needs. Their bloodline has grown thin from inbreeding."

They were interrupted by the arrival of Madam Belanger with some new gowns to be tried on. While the fittings were going forth, Lady Hadley shot a line off to Mrs. Comstock, notifying her that the Duke of Rutledge would be calling that afternoon. She feared that Helena might settle on the duke after all, and this was her little way of helping Edward out. Marion was no charmer, to be sure, yet she seemed a suitable sort of icicle for Rutledge. And in any case, the duke could not make any headway with that lump of a girl looking on.

73

Lady Helena had the pleasure of wearing a pretty new walking suit of mauve sarcenet for the duke's visit. As the day was fine, she hoped to enjoy a drive with him. She had her letter tucked into her reticule, in case they met Moira.

Mrs. Comstock and her daughter arrived a quarter of an hour before the duke. As there was company in the house, Rutledge did not like to scoop up Lady Helena and leave without a few moments' conversation with the other ladies. No sooner was his tea poured than Severn arrived.

"You are home early, Edward," his mama exclaimed.

"The House was quiet today. I thought I might be in time to meet the company if I returned early." Seeing Helena's quizzing smile, he turned to the Comstocks and added, "I am delighted you came to see us, Mrs. Comstock. And, of course, Marion. *Ça va sans dire.*"

Now that the party had been augmented, the duke felt freer to draw Lady Helena away. "Would you like to go out for a spin, Lady Helena? We are enjoying one of our rare fine days. It seems a shame to waste it."

Miss Comstock rose immediately. The duke frowned in confusion. "Actually, I am driving my curricle," he said, aiming his words at the grate, as he did not wish to offend Miss Comstock.

Severn set his cup down and said, "Let us take my carriage. We can all fit in it." He hardly knew why he had come scrambling home. He told himself he wanted to insure the duke's having a warm welcome, but this did not account for his dislike of Helena driving out alone with him.

"How nice," Helena said, with a sly look at Severn.

The drive was unsuccessful. Rutledge could make no headway in front of an audience. Marion addressed most of her conversation to Severn in a pointed way. Severn feared he had raised hopes in her breast that he had no intention of fulfilling. Such general conversation as occurred consisted of a few questions directed to Severn by Rutledge, rather curt replies, and a few comments on the passing scene for Helena's benefit. They were home within the hour.

"What have you seen of London thus far?" Rutledge asked Lady Helena as he escorted her to the door.

She mentioned the places Severn had shown her. "Churches and Parliament buildings and the Tower of London," she said with very little enthusiasm.

"Have you seen the horses at Astley's Circus?" he asked.

Marion, who had overheard the question, said, "Astley's Circus? Surely that is for children, Your Grace."

"I would love to see it! I adore performing horses," Lady Helena exclaimed.

"Then I shall take you tomorrow," Rutledge said. "I shan't invite you to join us, Miss Comstock, as you have already shown your displeasure." He had a few private words with Helena.

Miss Comstock was finessed and took out her ill humor on Severn. "Astley's Circus," she scoffed. "We have been overestimating Helena's idea of greatness. If it were not for the fact that she seems disinterested in the duke, I would think she accepted the invitation only to be alone with him."

"It is a pity you did not care to accompany them."

"I was not invited, Severn. Shabby manners!"

Rutledge left in restored spirits, and Severn pondered Helena's disinterest in the duke. Rutledge was a dull old fellow, when all was said and done. He would think of someone livelier for Helena. No hurry, the Season was just beginning.

Her disinterest was confirmed after the trip to Astley's.

"Did you enjoy your outing?" Severn inquired over dinner.

"The riders are very skilled. I cannot imagine how they maintain their balance, standing barefoot on the horses. I would have been satisfied with one show. However, Rutledge wanted to stay and see it all a second time. It would have been more interesting if we had been with a group. Perhaps Marion would like to come with us to Richmond Gardens tomorrow."

"You can ask her at Almack's this evening," Severn said.

Helena wondered at Mr. Malvern's delay in calling on her. Her first question upon returning from any outing was to ask whether she had had any callers. She left word with Sugden that if Mr. Malvern called, he was to leave a message. That seemed the easiest way out of the dilemma of his promised call. Severn had hinted that she ought not to see him, and she disliked to entertain him at Belgrave Square after that hint. If he left Moira's address, she would write him a thank-you note. If he asked for an interview, she would arrange to meet him away from the house. Now that she had her own carriage, this was by no means impossible.

His failure to come suggested that he had not yet

gotten any word on Mrs. Petrel-Jones. She could advertise, as Malvern had suggested, but then that would bring Moira to Belgrave Square, and the top-lofty Severn had also hinted that this was ineligible. Really, he was impossible! Was everyone in England so proud? What would Severn say when he learned that her papa planned to marry Moira? No doubt that would make *her* undesirable as well.

She felt, at times, as if she was living at Belgrave Square under false pretenses. She also felt that she was not executing her father's errand with the promptness and vigor that he expected and deserved. She knew there was virtually no chance of seeing Moira at dull, prestigious Almack's. Moira would not go, even in the unlikely event that she received a voucher. Orgeat and playing cards for chicken stakes were not her idea of an enjoyable evening.

The visit to Almack's went off much as she expected. It was a very proper affair. She stood up with Severn, and the duke, and a few similar types. The patronesses were pleased with her, and Lady Jersey gave her permission to waltz. That, at least, was good news, but when she returned home, she suffered a fit of the dismals.

Before retiring, she tiptoed to Lady Hadley's bed-chamber and said, "May I have a word with you, *Madrina*?"

Lady Hadley saw her worried little face and exclaimed, "You have had an offer from Rutledge! I knew it would come to this. My dear, I can see perfectly well that it has put you in the blue devils, but you need not fear. You do not have to accept him. Just say no, and we shan't tell anyone he offered."

"No, I did not let him ask me. I have discouraged him," she said, "for I could see his heart was more strongly engaged than mine. I told him it would not do. If we go out again, it will be as friends only."

"Is there someone else, then?" she asked fearfully.

Lady Helena sat on the edge of the bed and took her godmother's two hands. "I fear you will not like what I am about to say, *Madrina.* Indeed I fear you will ask me to leave when you hear—"

"Good God! You ain't enceinte!"

"*¿Qué?* What is 'enceinte'?"

"Never mind, dear. I am a foolish old lady. You could not possibly be, unless it happened before you left Spain or on the ship. In either case, it would not be *my* fault."

"The trouble is Papa," Helena said.

"You are missing him?"

"That, too, very much, but it is not missing him that troubles me at this moment. It is Mrs. Petrel-Jones," she said, and opened her budget to reveal her guilty secret. "So I must find her, yet Edward does not like me to see her or anyone who might know her. And if Papa marries her, then perhaps he will dislike that I stayed here without telling him of the connection. She is not considered déclassé in Spain, you understand. She was accepted everywhere, including at court."

"And she will be accepted here," Lady Hadley said, bridling up in defense of this stranger. "I never heard such nonsense. *I* am the mistress of this house, not Master Jackanapes Severn."

"Then may I put an advertisement in the journals and leave your house as my address?"

"Certainly you may. I shall make inquiries myself."

"Do you think Eduardo will be very angry?"

"I pay no heed to his sulks, but to avoid having to look at his Friday face, we shan't tell him. It is none of his business. We shall keep him in the dark for our own comfort. Now you go straight to your room and write up your notices. I shall have a footman take them around to all the journals in the morning."

"You are so very *simpática, Madrina.* How did you come to have such a proud son?"

"He takes after his papa. I cannot do a thing with Hadley either. That is why I run away to London alone every spring, to regain my fortitude for the long winter. I am too tired to argue about everything, so I just do as he says, but I also do what I please behind his back."

"It would have been better if you had bearded the lion at the beginning, *no es verdad?* A cub is easier to train than a fully grown lion."

"I ought to have put my foot down long ago. Any little thing the least bit out of the ordinary upsets him. He never wants me to change the curtains or furniture, or invite anyone new to dinner. I cannot imagine how he is not a Tory, except that the family have been Whigs forever, and he would not like to change."

It was not until Helena had returned to her bedchamber that Lady Hadley realized she had not pointed out that Edward was quite different from his papa. She hoped she had not given Helena the wrong idea. Really, those two would suit rather well. Unless two headstrong youngsters under one roof might lead to violence . . .

Chapter Nine

Severn had viewed the splendors of Richmond Hill many times in the past. When he learned that Marion was to accompany Helena and Rutledge on the outing, he felt no further chaperon was required. He was becoming wary of being too much in Marion's company. She was beginning to speak in a proprietary way of Severn and herself as "us," versus the "them" of the duke and Helena.

Richmond Hill was popular as an afternoon's outing to enjoy the Terrace Gardens, the water, and the pavilions, finishing with a stop at the Star and Garter Hotel for a well-earned tea. While awaiting a table, they strolled out to view the Italian-style garden of the hotel.

"Is it not beautiful?" Marion said, gazing at the panorama below. The Star and Garter was at the crest of the hill.

There was no gainsaying its beauty. The rolling hills, dotted with banks of flowers, were indeed breathtaking. But their beauty was of a tame sort that did not strike Helena as the very epitome of beauty. Something in her yearned for the starker grandeur of Spain. She found Richmond Hill reminded her of a beautiful English lady, made beautiful more by art and contrivance than by nature.

Even its art and contrivance lacked the bold stroke of Spain's. She preferred the rugged grandeur of nature's own mountains and sea.

Helena sighed nostalgically and said what was expected. "It is lovely. I have never seen anything quite like it before." She turned to smile her pleasure and saw Malvern staring at her over Marion's shoulder. He was with a mixed group of ladies and gentlemen.

As they all looked perfectly respectable, Helena did not hesitate to excuse herself for a moment and join them. "Mr. Malvern, I have been hoping you would call," she said, darting up to him.

He bowed gracefully. "Lady Helena! Now the view is complete. There was a—something lacking. You have added the coup de grace."

"Fine words, sir, but you do not distract me from my quest. Have you found Mrs. Petrel-Jones?"

"I planned to call later this afternoon. I have not forgotten your request, Lady Helena. I had no luck in discovering your friend's address, but I learned she is often to be found at a little coffee shop where the Spanish coterie meet. It is called El Cafeto. The émigrés meet there. I thought we might go there one morning."

She wished Malvern had gone there himself and discovered Moira'a address for her. His asking to take her could be an excuse to be with her, but he owed her nothing, after all. It was kind of him to have done this much, and as Lady Hadley was now aware of the situation, Helena agreed to go. The morning hour suited her. Severn usually went to the House in the morning. She could be home without his ever knowing she had gone.

"That is kind of you. What hour would be convenient?"

"Eleven o'clock tomorrow? Shall I call for you?"

"Yes, please," she said eagerly.

"Perhaps we could take your rig. I have not set up a carriage. I know you have your own, as I have seen you dashing along Bond Street, turning everyone's head. You are to be complimented on your prowess as a whip."

"Doing it too brown, Mr. Malvern. I am a very tyro. Would it be more convenient for me to meet you there?"

"Oh, no." He laughed. "If you have convinced your chaperon to let me darken the door, I shall call for you."

"You are too foolish." She laughed, embarrassed at accepting a favor from him when there was some doubt as to his being allowed to enter the house.

"I shall call on you at eleven sharp. You see how eager I am to win your approval. I do not usually arise until noon."

"You should be ashamed to own it, sir. That suggests you are out hell-raking till the small hours of the morning."

"You should try it sometime," he said daringly. "There are livelier dos than Almack's in London."

"You tempt me, Mr. Malvern. I look forward to seeing you at eleven tomorrow."

She left to rejoin her own party. Marion, she noticed, had edged closer to Malvern's group. Had she overheard the arrangements? No matter, she never came to call so early.

They were soon shown in to a table to enjoy a glass of wine and the Maid of Honor cheesecakes that were a feature of the hotel. Rutledge was an eager host and entertained the ladies as well as he could. Several young groups stopped to talk to them. With an outing to the theater to look forward to that evening, they then returned home.

"Perhaps you would be kind enough to take Miss Comstock home, Duke?" Helena said when they reached Belgrave Square.

"Mama is calling on Lady Hadley this afternoon. I am to meet her here," Marion said. The duke walked them to the door, hoping for a private word with Helena, but Marion stood her ground until he left.

"Would anyone mind very much if I take my siesta now?" Lady Helena said when they entered the saloon. "I have a slight migraine."

"In Spain, they take a nap every afternoon," Lady Hadley explained to the others. "They call it siesta. *Cousina* is teaching me Spanish, eh, *Cousina?*"

"You are making remarkable strides, ma'am."

"Sleep in the middle of the afternoon?" Mrs. Comstock exclaimed. "How do they ever get any work done?" She added aside to her hostess, "You want to break the gel of these foreign customs."

"Run along and have your siesta, *Cousina*," Lady Hadley said. "I find it a lovely idea, Audrey. I shall try it myself one of these days, when I am free of visitors." She looked hopefully to her guests, but they sat on.

Marion had revealed to her mama that Severn was a likelier prospect than Rutledge. Mrs. Comstock knew very well that Marion was aiming too high to hope for a ducal *parti* and lowered her sites accordingly. They both awaited Severn's return. When he arrived, his eyes scanned the room. "Where is Helena?" he asked.

"Having her siesta, Edward. She had a touch of migraine."

"Not serious, I hope?"

"No, no."

Marion's eager face told him she wanted to speak to him. She poured him a cup of tea and took it to a sofa, a little apart from the other ladies. "How was the outing to Richmond Hill?" he asked.

"Interesting. Lady Helena went darting off after a rackety crew of bucks. It was a Mr. Malvern that she spoke to."

A frown drew Severn's eyebrows together. "She met him at Lady Perth's ball. He is only after her fortune, of course."

"He did not seek her out. She went scrambling after him in an ill-bred way. Rutledge was shocked. Did you ever ask her about Moira? I mentioned that Spanish lady named Moira. I managed to get a peek in her reticule today. She has a letter for Moira. Very odd. I overheard Malvern mentioning something about the Spanish émigrés usually meeting somewhere. He is taking Helena there tomorrow. She did not ask me to join her."

"She is up to something, by God!"

"They are leaving at eleven. I shall call at ten-thirty."

"That is very kind of you, Marion. I appreciate your help in this matter. I would go myself, but—"

"You have more important matters to attend to than overseeing her carrying on. One hears you are doing fine work at the House." She smiled, taking this as an effort to please her. "I am happy to assist you, Edward."

She had never called him Edward before. It sounded worrisome on her lips. The whole affair had a conspiratorial air about it that he disliked. It was interfering of Marion to have looked in Helena's reticule. Yet Malvern was certainly up to no good. Helena must be protected from her own naïveté.

"Between us, we shall hint her in the duke's direction," she said complacently. "We shall let them sit together at the theater tonight. Your mama has invited me and Mama. You and I will sit in the back of the box. It will be more—private," she said daringly.

Severn laughed nervously. "The duke is a tame enough fellow. No fear of his getting out of line. You ladies will like to sit in the front seats."

At the theater, however, Miss Comstock had her way. She stopped at the back seats and drew Severn down beside her. "I do not mind sitting in the back, Edward," she said. "We will be able to overhear everything they say from here."

Severn flinched at this calculating speech. The other couple's conversation was easily overheard in the small box, but it was hardly worth listening to. Rutledge's first disappointment at the unprepossessing physical appearance of Kean soon turned to praise. "A demmed fine performance." Lady Helena agreed with the rest of London that Kean could deliver a rant with the best of them.

They went to the Clarendon for supper after the performance. Over a braised guinea hen, Rutledge said, "Now that you have seen our professional ranters, Lady Helena, would you like to visit the House tomorrow morning and hear the amateurs?"

"I'm afraid I have a previous appointment, Duke," she said, and immediately rushed on to speak of other things.

Marion gave a sapient nod in Severn's direction.

"I shall let you know what transpires," she said in a low voice.

"Very kind," he said, falling deeper into her debt.

Helena observed the growing closeness between Severn and Marion and wondered at it. *Were* they in love?

Lady Hadley retired as soon as their carriage reached Belgrave Square. Severn poured two glasses of wine and handed Helena one. "How did you enjoy Richmond Hill?" he asked.

"Spain has spoiled me for such tame beauty, but I thanked the duke very prettily."

"You and Rutledge are rubbing along well, I take it?"

"He is tolerably amusing," she allowed, then gave him a knowing look. "If you are hatching plans for a wedding between us, however, I must disillusion you. I will not marry him."

"Has he asked you already!"

"No, I did not permit him to ask, for I dislike refusing. If you were counting on him to get me off your hands, Eduardo, your plan has not worked." She spoke lightly, but he sensed an undercurrent of anger. She could not possibly know his plan.

"Why, we are in no hurry to lose you, Cousin." He smiled. "We are just getting to know each other."

Again she smote him with a sharp look. "There you are mistaken, my friend. You have not begun to know me yet at all. *You* may feel obliged to marry where your father decrees; *I* shall marry where I wish, and I shall not hide behind anyone's skirts to do it."

"I don't understand."

She measured him with a cool look. "I think you

do, Severn. You cannot be unaware of our fathers' wish that we marry. Why else was I sent that miniature likeness of you?"

"What miniature? I know nothing of it." His frown dwindled to a sneer. "Odd you mistook me for Sugden when you arrived, as you were apparently familiar with my face."

Caught dead to rights, she had to admit it. "I was angry that you apparently did not recognize a lady when you saw one. Your whole behavior in not having me met at the boat was nothing less than an insult. I think you did it on purpose. You do not wish to marry me, and rather than tell your father so, you tried to give me a disgust of you. That is pusillanimous behavior. You hide behind my skirts, leaving it for me to be the one to refuse."

"How can you refuse when I have not offered and have no intention of doing so?"

"Have you told your father this?"

"Of course not."

"Then you are a coward, sir. I see precisely what you are about, trying to palm me off on Rutledge while you appear to be doing Hadley's bidding by escorting me here and there in a halfhearted way. I would think better of you if you stood up like a man and told your father and *me* that you do not care for the match. That is what a gentleman would do. Are you a puppy, to be afraid of a little scolding for disobedience?"

Severn felt culpable when the matter was put into these blunt terms, but if Helena knew his papa, she would realize "a little scolding" did not begin to describe his rages. Of course, Severn was not about to admit to his behavior. "I am sorry if you have found my efforts to entertain you unsatisfactory,

Cousin. In the face of your total disinterest, I can hardly see that it matters."

She did not stamp her foot, but she looked as if she would like to. "What matters is your cowardice. I told my father I would marry where I wished, and I do not wish to marry you, so your paltry schemes were unnecessary."

"Then you have no reason to complain at my lack of ardor, if that is what has caused this outburst."

"I do not want your ardor!" she exclaimed haughtily. "What would an Englishman know of ardor? You *ingléses* have ice water in your veins. What I am complaining of is your duplicity."

"Where is the necessity for duplicity when you have told me you would refuse an offer?"

"Yes, but you had no way of knowing that, had you? I have always behaved with warm friendship toward you."

"Why was that, I wonder, as you did not wish to marry me?"

A flush rose up her neck. "We are cousins. I hoped we might be friends," she said.

"You hoped I would offer for you," he said firmly.

Her eyes grew large in outrage. Her nostrils pinched, and her breath came in gasps. Severn couldn't make heads or tails of the spate of Spanish that flew from her lips, but he understood the anger in her words. He also appreciated the beauty of her flashing eyes. The girl was part wildcat. "Hope for an offer!" she said, switching to English. "I hoped for no more than to keep you biddable, but that is not necessary after all. It is your mama who is my chaperon."

"And you have done a sterling job of ingratiating *her*!"

"How dare you imply I am insincere!"

"Emptying the butter boat on us to insure our good humor does not qualify as sincerity in my books."

"But I love *Madrina*! I was never insincere with *her*!"

"Only with me," he said, with a quizzing look. "We have a saying in English, having to do with the pot calling the kettle black. We are neither of us snow-white in this affair, Cousin. Now that the ground is cleared, there is no need for simulation between us either, is there? You do not wish to marry me. I do not wish to marry you. Perhaps we can now become true friends."

Helena considered this a moment, then said, "*Sí*," in a grudging way. When he moved to refill her glass, she withdrew it. "I shall retire now. Good night, Severn."

"My name is still Eduardo." He reached for her hand and squeezed it lightly. "Friends?"

"*Sí*," she said reluctantly, and left.

Her hot Spanish soul would have relished a more passionate argument. The *ingléses* understood neither love nor hatred. Not that she hated Eduardo, precisely. She only hated his resorting to reason in the heat of argument. He should have been either straining at the leash to strike her—she would have enjoyed egging him on, knowing he was helpless to retaliate—or he should have swept her into his arms for a passionate embrace. That would also have been a satisfactory conclusion to their argument. But only if they were in love, of course. Which they were not.

At least they were now friends. A female friend of her own age would have been more satisfactory.

Marion would never be her friend. Marion hovered over her life like a shadow that cast an air of gloom. Helena had the strange sensation of being constantly observed, as if she were a criminal suspect.

Ah, well, tomorrow morning she would escape the Argus-eyed Marion and meet a few people from Spain. That would be amusing, and hopefully she would find Moira.

Chapter Ten

Helena waited until Severn had left in the morning before telling Lady Hadley her plans. "You have no objection to my going with Mr. Malvern to El Cafeto, *Madrina*?"

"Doesn't it sound exotic! El Cafeto. What is an El Cafeto, my dear? It is not something shady, I hope?"

"It can be shady," Helena replied mischievously. "The words mean 'the coffee tree,' but in this case, it is the name of a coffee shop."

"Ah, tree, shade—I catch your little pun. Good gracious, there can be no harm in *that*. The gentlemen used to keep the coffee shops for themselves, but everyone goes now."

"I shouldn't be longer than an hour."

"I shall write to Hadley this morning. He suspects I am enjoying myself if I don't keep him informed."

"Ah, we would not want him to suspect the worst." Helena smiled.

Lady Hadley, determined to do her duty as a chaperon, was in her saloon to meet Mr. Malvern before turning Helena over to him. She found no fault in either his manners or appearance.

"I shall take good care of your charge, ma'am," he assured her before leaving.

"Enjoy yourself at El Cafeto," the dame said. "I may have a little siesta after I write my letter, *Cousina*."

"*Buenos días*," Malvern said, and made his exiting bow.

As they reached the door, a knock sounded on it. "Who can that be?" Helena asked.

Sugden opened the door to admit Mrs. Comstock and Marion. They did not say, "Aha!" but they looked it.

"Going out so early, Lady Helena?" Mrs. Comstock inquired, her eyes running up and down poor Mr. Malvern as though he were a wild beast at Exeter Exchange.

"As you see, ma'am, I am just leaving. I hope you will still be here when I return. I shan't be long." Her hope was to get out without introducing Mr. Malvern.

"You have not introduced us to your beau," Marion said.

"Mr. Malvern is not my beau," Helena said coolly, "but by all means let me introduce you." She made the introduction.

Malvern behaved himself like a gentleman and said he was charmed to make their acquaintance. Ever on the alert for an heiress, he gave Marion a special smile and said he was sure he had seen her before. One did not soon forget such beauty.

When Marion, unaccustomed to such flattery, made a simpering smile, her mama prodded her in the back with her fist and said, "Marion will go with you, Helena. That is why we called, so that you would have an escort for your drive."

"I already have an escort, thank you all the same. Lady Hadley will be so happy you are here."

"Go with them, Marion," the dame said, and that was that.

Malvern, who was accustomed to tight corners, kept up a lively flow of nonsense while Helena steered her tilbury through the morning traffic on Piccadilly. He directed her to Haymarket, then to Orange Street, where the El Cafeto flourished, or at least survived, in England's cooler clime.

Malvern was an excellent cohort. When Marion asked where they were going, he said, "Your cousin became homesick to hear a Spanish voice, so I told her of a certain spot. She feared she would never find it, and she accepted my escort. I hope you enjoy it, too, Miss Comstock. It is something a little out of the ordinary. That is what is so fascinating about London, is it not? One can find anything, if one looks hard enough." He allowed his wicked eyes to flicker over her sluglike face and added, "Even the perfect lady."

Marion was by no means sure she wanted to find such a place as the El Cafeto. It was small, dark, noisy, and crowded with people, mostly men, in strange clothes.

Malvern found them a table. "Perhaps you had best speak to the waiter, Lady Helena," he said. "I would say my Spanish is rusty, except that I don't have any to have rusted. You will know what to ask for." His glance suggested more than food.

She ordered coffee and cakes, and as the language ensured privacy, she also inquired for Señora Petrel-Jones, an *inglesa*.

"Ah, *sí*." The waiter knew of the señora. She

93

came frequently but was not here this morning. Was there a message?

Helena preferred to deliver her papa's letter herself, but she scribbled off a note while Malvern entertained Marion.

"What was that you were writing, Helena?" Marion asked as soon as the waiter left.

"I have ordered some coffee to take home with me," she lied. "The waiter gave directions how to make it."

"I see," Marion said. She had not heard the name Moira, but she meant to see if that letter had left the reticule.

The waiter had apparently spread word that Lady Helena was among them, for several dark-visaged men stopped at the table and shouted in unnecessarily loud voices. There was a deal of laughing, and even some tears—from men! Marion looked to Malvern for condemnation. He shrugged his handsome shoulders.

"The Spanish are so emotional," he said.

One man, very handsome except that he wore a gaudy green jacket and a Belcher kerchief in lieu of a proper cravat, was particularly persistent. When he left, Helena said, "Juan is from Andalusia, my home district. They are famous for their guitar music there. He is going to play us a song."

Juan stood on a table and strummed his instrument. His voice was deep and rich, and his black eyes gleamed like oil as he sang straight to Helena. Marion could not understand the words, but she knew what *amor* meant, at least. She also could see that Helena was having difficulty controlling her feelings. She did not cry, but her eyes were glazed with unshed tears.

Marion felt a curious softness grow inside herself, too, as the plangent music hung on the still air. It excited a strange longing inside her. The shadowy room, the dark faces and liquid eyes, and especially the strumming guitar throbbed with passion. No wonder Helena was so different, growing up amidst this turbulence. How cold and stark England must seem to her.

When the song was finished, the room shook with applause. Helena rose and went to speak with Juan. Marion watched closely as she opened her reticule. The letter did not come out, however. What she was doing was giving Juan money. Really!

"Surely it was not up to you, a lady, to give him a pourboire," Marion said when Helena returned.

"It was not a pourboire, but a gift. Juan hopes to bring his family from Spain. He is having difficulty finding work."

"What does he do?" Malvern asked idly.

"He is a musician. He plays beautifully, does he not? And he composes his own music. I shall ask Lady Hadley if he might play a few numbers at my ball. One never knows. It might catch on and bring him more customers to raise the necessary funds."

Helena seemed strangely eager to leave as soon as the music was over. She remembered to ask the waiter (in Spanish) if she might buy a bag of coffee, to allay Marion's suspicions. He filled her request with no difficulty.

When they rose to leave, Helena managed to whisper aside to Malvern, "I must speak to you a moment alone."

From El Cafeto they drove directly home, with no chance for privacy. Marion was strangely lethargic, even for her, but she was not entirely comatose. Helena feared she would rouse herself if she suspected anything. They reached Belgrave Square without the desired privacy having been achieved.

Desperate, Lady Helena said, "Won't you come inside for a moment, Mr. Malvern?"

He agreed, but doubtfully. When they were inside, Helena set aside her bonnet and said, "Will you tell Lady Hadley we are home, Marion? I want to speak with Malvern about hiring Juan for my party. Perhaps Juan does not do that sort of thing."

Malvern donned his most charming smile and turned to Marion. "It has been a great pleasure to finally meet you, Miss Comstock. I hope it will not be long before we meet again."

"I look forward to it, Mr. Malvern," she said, with a rare smile of genuine pleasure.

As soon as she was gone, he said to Helena, "What is it?"

"What are you doing tonight?" she asked.

"I have cards to half a dozen routs."

"To Lady Mobrey's ball?"

"Alas, I do not fly so high."

"Which routs?" she asked, and he named a few.

"Mrs. Stephen's, you say. We have cards for it. I shall manage to get to Mrs. Stephen's do around eleven. I want you to take me somewhere. Just a flying visit, and we shall return to the rout. Will you do it, Mr. Malvern?"

"Am I likely to end up at the Court of Twelve Paces with Lord Severn? You may think these hole-and-corner affairs are nothing to a man like me. You are quite mistaken. Gentlemen in my tenuous position are as closely watched as a deb. You are charming, milady, but you are not likely to marry me, and I cannot have you blackening my fair name."

"Juan told me Mrs. Petrel-Jones has purchased a ticket for a masquerade ball in aid of the Spanish émigrés. I want to attend and give her my father's letter."

"I'll deliver it for you," he said at once.

She hesitated. Malvern was kind and helpful, but he did not share her sense of urgency. "I would prefer to go myself."

"Surely Severn would take you. There can be nothing amiss in your wanting to attend such a do."

"Oh, but I do not want Severn along, asking questions. And besides, it is not the sort of thing he would approve of. It will be a rowdy affair, I fear. It is a public ball with sold tickets. I bought two dozen, as I feared Juan would not accept charity. You know the sort of hurly-burly affair it will be."

"Very well, I'll take you, but if trouble arises, you must do the gentlemanly thing and protect me. We shall require dominoes and masks. I'll take care of that."

She took his hand and squeezed it. "How can I thank you?"

"I'll think of something." He bowed and took his leave.

Lady Helena joined the ladies, expecting questions on her unusual outing. As it turned out, Marion had already given a satisfactory account. The only questions had to do with hiring Juan for her ball, and with the coffee she had purchased.

Mrs. Comstock said, "It sounds an odd sort of morning, but there is no harm in broadening one's horizons, after all. Do not hesitate to include Marion in such outings another time, Helena. She will be happy to accompany you. Malvern is some kin to the Beauforts, you say, Marion?"

"On his mama's side," Marion said.

It seemed that Malvern, without a feather to fly with and no real claim to distinction, had passed inspection. He had had the insight to recognize a lady of rare beauty and accomplishments in Marion, and so he was allowed to be eligible.

The Comstocks soon took their leave. Severn did not return directly home that day. Curious as to Helena's outing, he stopped at South Audley Street to ask Marion for an account.

"You worried for nothing, Edward," Marion said. "Malvern took us to a Spanish café for Helena to meet some Spaniards."

"Travel is broadening," Mrs. Comstock informed him, for it was not to be supposed Marion met Severn without a chaperon. "They heard Spanish music, accompanied by guitar. Marion says it was quite moving. Lady Helena speaks of hiring Juan somebody to play for her ball."

"She will make a laughingstock of herself, and you tell me it is nothing to worry about!" Severn exclaimed.

"I met Mr. Malvern," Mrs. Comstock announced. "He is well mannered. Marion says he behaved very properly."

"Of course he behaved properly, to lure the ladies into thinking him fit for decent society. His pockets are to let. He is sniffing around only in hopes of claiming Helena's fortune."

"Actually, he was very attentive to Marion," Mrs. Comstock said with a sage nod. She hoped to convey the notion that Severn had best look sharp if he hoped to win the prize.

"That must give you cause for concern. Marion's ten thousand would be a boon to the likes of Malvern."

"I don't say Marion will be allowed to go out with him, but he is seen everywhere. There can be no harm in standing up with him at a ball or rout."

"I would not advise you to permit anything of the sort," he said, and rose in a huff to take his leave.

"Severn is developing green eyes, I think," the mother said sagely. "Malvern can be put to good use. If he is at Lady Mobrey's ball tonight, you may give him a dance, Marion."

"I asked him if he would be there. He is attending Mrs. Stephen's rout. We have cards for it as well."

"We are promised to the ball, but we shall make Severn stop in at the rout for a moment. We cannot hurt dear Mrs. Stephen's feelings by not showing up. Lady Hadley will not be going with us this evening. She has some cronies coming in for cards, so I am chaperoning you girls. I fancy Severn will want to stand up with you twice this evening, Marion. I shall not allow it, of course, until he has come up to scratch."

Marion listened to this complacently. She wondered if Mr. Malvern would want two dances.

Chapter Eleven

Lord Severn's annoyance had risen to a fevered pitch by the time he reached Belgrave Square. He had warned Helena away from Malvern, and what did she do? Invite the scoundrel to his house. She had gone with him to a foreign den to hire a guitar strummer to play at her ball. Was this the way to treat a friend? It was time he let her know who ran this household.

"Send Lady Helena to my study at once," he growled at Sugden as he handed him his curled beaver and York tan gloves.

"Yes, your lordship."

The message was relayed down the hierarchy of servants. By the time Sally delivered it to her mistress's ears, it had reached alarming proportions.

"His lordship's sore as a gumboil, milady, and demands you go to his study this instant, if you know what's good for you."

Lady Helena's gore rose at this command. She lifted a nail file and began nonchalantly filing her nails.

"He said right away," Sally reminded her.

"I heard you, Sally. Would you mind brushing my hair?"

"He's waiting, *now*!"

"Let him wait," Helena said, and handed Sally the brush.

After her hair had been brushed to a high gloss, she took up a bottle of perfume and dabbed it behind her ears. She went to the clothespress and selected a fringed shawl, which she arranged with elaborate concern over her shoulders.

A knock at the door interrupted her toilette. It was Agnes, the upstairs maid. "His lordship's waiting for you in his study, milady," she said, her eyes bulging. "He's pacing and twitching his tail like a mad lion."

"I shall be down presently, Agnes," Lady Helena said unconcernedly. Then she sat down and filed her nails again for five minutes. She rose slowly, smoothed her gown, and descended to Severn's study. Her heart was not palpitating, nor was she pale with fear, but there was a steely glint in her dark eyes.

Severn stopped his pacing and turned a scowl on her. "It's about time you got here. I sent for you twenty minutes ago."

"I suggest you word your request more civilly next time, milord. I am a poor hand at executing *orders*." She sat in the chair by the desk and arranged her skirt about her, then lifted her chin and asked coolly, "Now, what is this urgent matter that has interrupted my toilette?"

"The urgent matter is your outing with Malvern. I told you I did not want him seeing you."

"I remember your mentioning that he did not please you, milord. He finds acceptance with me, however. And with your good friends, the Comstocks, I might add."

"It is no mitigation of the offense that you dragged Marion into it."

"I did not *drag* her, I assure you. She pitched herself into the carriage uninvited. There was no escaping her."

"I understand the crowd at this Spanish café consisted mostly of men—foreign men, at that."

"No need to ask where you get your information. Obviously you have not spoken to the despised Mr. Malvern."

"No, but by God, I shall. He has a lot of gall taking you there."

She rose imperiously from her chair and directed a hard stare at him. "I asked him to take me. By all means, vent your spleen on me, Severn. I am not afraid of your little squalls. But I will not have you read a lecture to my friends. And don't think you are weaseling out of having set Marion to watch me. Why else did you go running to her before coming home?"

"I happened to be passing South Audley Street—"

"You were not passing South Audley Street on your way home from Westminster. I am no longer a total stranger to the thoroughfares of London."

Caught dead to rights, he did not defend, but attacked the harder. "I will not have Malvern in my house."

"*Your* house, milord? I had not heard of your father's demise. Lady Hadley is mistress of this establishment, and my chaperon." She bit back the information that Lady Hadley was aware of the outing. Let the poor lady have her peace. There was no need of assistance in handling Severn.

"You pull the wool over Mama's eyes. You don't fool me."

"And just what do you think I am trying to fool you about, Severn?" she demanded. "I asked Mr. Malvern to take me to a Spanish café because I was lonesome. I wanted to hear a voice from home. I think you might have done as much if you had been in Spain without hearing English for some time. Marion accompanied me. What is your objection? She enjoyed herself thoroughly, to judge by her simpering at Malvern. Perhaps *that* is what riles you!"

"I am indeed riled that you are debauching a young lady."

"She is half a decade older than I, and if sipping coffee is considered debauchery, then there is no hope for England. The crime in my opinion is that we are forced to drink tea."

"Spanish cafés may do well enough for you, Cousin. You have lived abroad and seen something of the world. Marion has led a tamer sort of life. I would appreciate your keeping her out of such adventures in the future. I would very strongly advise that you not develop any close relationship with Malvern. To say Mama is your chaperon is mere quibbling. While under this roof, you are under my protection. I repeat, I do not want Malvern coming to this house. It leaves the impression I approve of him. I do not. If he is so unwise as to ask for your hand, I shall tell him precisely why."

"I see your real concern is for Marion," she said, with a toss of her curls. "I shall be more than happy to exclude her, if you can convince her she is not welcome. God knows it has never stopped her in the past."

"My concern is not only . . . not mostly for Marion. Her mother is in charge of her conduct, though

103

I should dislike to see her fall into poor company on your account."

"Very well, Severn. You do not wish to see Mr. Malvern at Belgrave Square. As a guest in the house, I must accede to your request. I shall take care that he does not return, and I promise you I shall let Marion know your feelings. Was there anything else you wished to get off your chest?"

Severn did not feel he had gotten anything off his chest thus far. Indeed the burden seemed to have increased. He could see as clear as glass that Lady Helena was in the boughs, and a Lady Helena in such a mood was capable of anything.

"It is not my intention to cramp your style, Cousin," he said more gently. "London offers sufficient proper amusements that one need not go out of the way to find improper ones."

"You are quite mistaken to think that Spanish ladies and gentlemen are less proper than their English counterparts. I was never out of sight of my *dueña* with a gentleman, and if I had been, it would have made no difference in his behavior. It seems the English gentlemen are less trustworthy. I shall bear it in mind, milord. Now if there is nothing more . . ."

"One more item. About this Juan fellow. It will not do to have guitar music at your ball. No one would know how to dance to such foreign tunes."

"One does not usually dance at a concert. I meant to have a short musical interlude, perhaps at the supper hour, for listening only."

"Hardly to guitar music, surely!"

"Don't display your horrid English prejudice," she sniffed. "You mock something you have never heard. I suggest you go to El Cafeto and hear some *real* music. It might do you a world of good."

His reply surprised her. "Where would I find this Cafeto?"

"On Orange Street off Haymarket. Be prepared to drink real coffee, not tea. That is something else that will astonish your deliquescent taste buds."

"I frequently drink coffee."

"Not Spanish coffee. It is like the Spanish race—stronger and more flavorful than the English variety."

"You find us dull?"

"Even when you think you are being ferocious," she said, smiling. "Poor Eduardo. You would not frighten a kitten. But perhaps your little temper will keep Marion in line." With a bold smile, she left the room.

Severn watched her depart, her head high and her stride easy. Her skirts swayed in a seductive manner unlike that of English ladies' skirts. He was far from feeling he had had the better of their encounter. She had not promised not to see Malvern, only not to bring him to the house, which was more dangerous than seeing him here.

He understood that she might be lonesome for some echo of Spain. Perhaps he had been too hard on her. He would make it a point to take her to the Spanish café one of these days, to show her his heart was in the right place. At least he could be easy in his mind tonight. There was little likelihood that Malvern would have a ticket to Lady Mobrey's ball. On this self-deluding thought, he went abovestairs to make his toilette.

Chapter Twelve

Lord Severn's party, including the Comstocks and a few dozen other elite, was invited to dinner at Lady Mobrey's before her ball. This was convenient to Helena's plan, as it meant an early attendance at the ball and a possibility of removing to Mrs. Stephen's rout at eleven. Helena expected to find Severn in the boughs after their argument and determined to have him back in humor before eleven. To this end, she made a toilette designed to please him. Her white gown was a model of propriety. Sally brushed her curls to a gloss and set a diamond-studded butterfly among them. A modest string of pearls hung at her throat. She felt she looked a perfect dowd.

She wore her most ingratiating smile when she descended the staircase and was surprised to see Severn wearing a similar face. Far from being on his high ropes, he seemed determined to cajole her into humor as well.

"Lovely, as usual, Cousin," he said, taking her hand at the bottom of the stairs. That he was there awaiting her was already an indication of approval. When he was out of sorts, he waited in the saloon with his mama.

"I hope I have not kept you waiting, Eduardo," she said, knowing full well she was early.

"On the contrary, we have time for a glass of sherry before leaving to pick up the Comstocks."

They had their sherry with Lady Hadley and the party she had invited to dine with her. Helena made the rounds of the company, having a few words with each of the elderly guests. At the appointed time, she and Severn left to pick up the Comstocks. Helena did not mention Mrs. Stephen's rout, but she had the invitations in her reticule. She would "remember" it just before eleven and suggest they drop in for a moment.

The last person she expected to assist her was Mrs. Comstock, and again she was surprised. The Comstocks were no sooner in the carriage than the dame said, "I hope you have brought along your cards for Mrs. Stephen's rout, Severn. We must drop in there for a bit after Mobrey's do."

"Why do you want to go there?" he asked. "Mobrey's will be more interesting."

"I cannot offend Mrs. Stephen. We work together on many charity affairs. I have assured her we shall attend."

Helena casually opened her reticule. "I believe I have the cards here," she said. "Yes, that was fortunate."

"No harm to drop in for a moment," Severn agreed, and the thing was done.

Helena planned to have her duty dance with Severn at the ball to insure being free of him at Stephen's rout. As they sat side by side at dinner, she tried to arrange it then.

"As you will be having the opening minuet with Marion, Eduardo, I want to claim you for the second set. May I put you down on my card for the cotillion?"

"Why not for the minuet?" he asked, flattered at her eagerness but a little chagrined that she assumed he owed Marion the first dance.

"I just assumed you and Marion would—"

"I have not asked her. You are my houseguest. Put me down for the minuet."

"But her feelings will be hurt, Eduardo. No, no. I will not set myself up as competition for Cousin Marion."

"Good God, you sound as though I were courting her."

She gave him a saucy smile. "Are you not? She is constantly at Belgrave Square."

"I asked her to drop by to be company for you."

"Too kind. Do you also call on her after work on my behalf? I assure you I am not that enamored of the lady. And I promise you she does not like me above half."

Severn already suspected where Marion's thoughts were heading. To hear confirmed that others suspected it frightened him to death. "Put me down for the minuet," he said firmly.

She drew out her dance book and entered his name. "I took a book as I entered and have already lined up all the most eligible gentlemen. Until eleven, my book is full. I know Mrs. Comstock wishes to leave early."

"Twelve is early enough, I think."

"That late?" she asked. "The rout will not last as long as the ball. I think we should arrive earlier, Eduardo."

"Perhaps you are right," he said, with a mischievous smile. "And you may put me down for the first dance at Mrs. Stephen's do as well."

Helena laughed at his trickery. "I see a new trend for young couples here. They might have every dance together by the simple expedient of dashing to all the parties, having one dance at each."

"Where else are we invited this evening?" he asked.

"To several other dos, but I brought only Mrs. Stephen's cards with me. In any case, mere friends do not monopolize each other's dance card. And now we really must have a word with our other partner, or we will be taken for yahoos."

Severn turned his conversation to Marion, and Helena to a Lord Depuis, on her other side. She was a little concerned about that dance with Severn at Stephen's rout, but it would be the first dance. He would have no reason to keep an eye on her after they had had their dance. As soon as it was over, she would seek Malvern out.

Mrs. Mobrey's ball was lovely. Her ballroom was decorated with flowers and had a maypole in the center. All the ton were there. Helena was much sought after. The only displeasure she caused was when she had to turn down several partners due to her early departure. Perhaps Miss Comstock was a little miffed not to have the minuet with Severn, but she had the cotillion and made do with that. She, too, spent the better part of one of the Season's major balls anticipating her departure.

Severn's party took their leave of the hostess at the appointed hour. She parted with them reluctantly, but her ball could truthfully be called a "squeeze," and no hostess could ask more than that.

The Stephen's rout was a sad comedown. The

house was smaller and less grand, the orchestra dwindled from a dozen musicians to four, and the refreshments from champagne to orgeat and punch. Most worrying of all, Helena feared that her absence would be noticed in the thinly populated rooms. Soon another fear came to goad her. There was little likelihood of Malvern not being spotted by Severn in this small group.

She looked around the room for Mr. Malvern and was attacked by yet another fear. One look confirmed that he was not there. The Comstocks also seemed to be looking for someone.

"Perhaps he is in the card parlor," Mrs. Comstock said aside to Marion. "I shall root him out." Marion went with her.

Severn turned to Helena. "Time for our second dance, Cousin."

"No, no, Eduardo. Our first dance at this rout. You will be putting ideas in folks' heads if we are seen standing up together twice."

"Oh, it is a country dance," he said, disappointed that it was to be a free-for-all, with no privacy. He had hoped for a waltz, now that Helena had been given permission by Almack's to indulge this vice. "Perhaps we should wait. . . ."

"You don't sound very eager to dance with me," she said, adopting a moue to distract him. Then she put her hand in his and drew him on to the floor.

The exigencies of the romp demanded most of her attention, but she noticed between steps that the room was filling up, and she was happy for it. It seemed that Mrs. Stephen's rout was not on the top of anyone's list, but as the evening wore on, folks hopped from one party to another, and Mrs. Stephen was well enough thought of that her do was included on their list.

Her wandering eye also noticed that Marion had latched on to Malvern. Wouldn't Severn be in the boughs if he saw that! Whenever his head turned in their direction, Helena was quick to divert him. She managed to catch Malvern's eye herself, however, and nodded toward the door, hoping he would realize she wanted to meet him there.

As soon as the dance was over, she said, "These country dances are death on a lady's toilette. I must freshen up. You may have another dance with Marion now, Eduardo."

"I rather thought I might ask the pretty blonde chatting with Mrs. Stephen to stand up with me." Severn was not trying to make Helena jealous. He only wished to put out of her mind the notion that he and Marion were romantically involved.

Helena did feel a little twinge of annoyance. The blonde was very pretty. But accomplishing her errand took priority, and to that end she said, "But you *will* stand up with Marion again. She might take a miff if you don't." That would keep him occupied for two sets, long enough to go to the Spanish ball and get back, if all went well.

She made her way to the door. Seeing no sign of Malvern, she kept going, in case Severn was watching. She found Malvern lurking in the hallway.

"What are we to use for a carriage?" were his first words.

She stared at him in dismay. "Did you not bring one?"

"I don't have one. I thought you would bring yours."

"No, I came with Severn. Oh, dear! We shall have

to hire a hansom cab. Let us go at once. You have the dominoes?"

"They are stashed in a bag in a small, dark parlor. I said I was leaving for a country visit immediately after the ball."

"How resourceful of you! But we cannot leave together. I shall slip out by a side door and meet you in the street. We must hurry, or our absence will be noticed."

"I've had a look around. There's a door to the outside in the small parlor. We can both leave unnoticed from there."

"You have done this sort of thing before!" She laughed.

"Not with a deb," he said, obviously worried.

They sneaked into the parlor when no one was looking and then out the side door together. They donned their dominoes outside the door before going into the street. They had to walk a block before an empty hansom cab passed and was hailed.

"I don't know what Mrs. Comstock would say if she heard of this," Malvern grouched as the coach rumbled toward the café.

"Are you setting your cap for Miss Comstock?" she inquired with interest.

"No, but I have a suspicion she is cocking her bonnet at me. I hope it is the case. She has ten thousand."

"Oh, Malvern! Really! Would you marry for such a reason?"

"Why not? The rest of the world does. I shall offend you by hinting it is not only your *beaux yeux* that have all the gentlemen in a flap, but I think your beauty is only half the reason. All the world knows you have a dot of twenty-five thousand pounds."

"Are you suggesting the Duke of Rutledge, with four palatial estates, is—"

"Actually, I was thinking of Severn. He is like a dog with a bone when he is with you. Severn is renowned for his way with shillings and pence, you must know. Brougham did not make him financial critic for no reason."

"There is nothing between Severn and me!" she exclaimed. Yet he had harped on Malvern's empty pockets. And, of course, he knew to a penny how much she had. He had been quite eager to take over her finances from Lady Hadley. She stored up Malvern's idle comment for future consideration.

"It ain't for any lack of trying on his part. He'd snap your dowry up fast enough if you gave him half a chance. And so would I snap up Marion's. Such a match would be the making of me. If I had ten thousand behind me, I could stand for Parliament. It would not be long before I made my way."

"But do you love her?"

"How can you love someone you don't know? I like her well enough. She is an intelligent, agreeable lady. I don't know how the world wags in Spain, but in England, I would be a fool not to have her if I could."

"If it is only a seat in Parliament you want, perhaps—"

"That is not a paying position, Lady Helena. A man needs a few shekels to live. The honorarium of a free frank for his letters doesn't go far."

Helena thought of the expenses he had occurred on her behalf and felt guilty. "Of course, I shall reimburse you for the domino and the hire of the cab," she said apologetically.

He patted her hand. "If I were a propertied gentleman, I would not permit it, but unless you want to walk back to Mrs. Stephen's house, I fear this must be a dutch outing."

"Poor Malvern," she said, then fell silent. Her mind was busy thinking of ways to help him. Ways that did not involve his having to marry Marion.

Before long, they reached Orange Street, where a motley crew of costumed revelers in the street told them the ball was nearby. A hand-painted banner over a doorway led them to the spot. Music came from an open doorway. "This must be it," she said. "Do you have the tickets?"

"I have the two dozen you bought from Juan," he said, patting his pocket as he assisted her from the carriage.

Chapter Thirteen

They entered a dark doorway and were confronted with a narrow staircase. The music came from above. They joined the throng mounting the stairs, the music and voices growing louder as they drew closer to the source.

"You shouldn't be here," Malvern said, worried. "Damn, I don't feel any too safe myself. Best put on your mask." They both did so.

"Don't be foolish. There is no danger. This is how the *campesinos* celebrate in Spain. Papa has often taken me to such affairs. Our grape pickers and field-workers had such parties at harvest time. The aristocracy have much duller parties."

A man wearing a devil's suit took their tickets and said, *"Bienvenido, señor y señorita."*

They passed into the long, dim room. It was hung with garish orange, yellow, and green streamers. All manner of costume was there. There were ladies in Spanish gowns from the last century, accompanied by their cavaliers. There were shepherdesses and one balding, rotund man in the rig of Henry VIII, wearing a satin tunic and long silk stockings.

"I shall never recognize Mrs. Petrel-Jones!" Helena said.

"And how will she recognize you?"

"That is simple enough. I shall remove my mask," she said, and took it off. "Don't worry, Malvern. There will be no one from the ton here to recognize me. Let us circulate amid the throng and hope Moira sees us."

Before she had gone three yards, a respectable-looking older gentleman in a plain black domino and mask accosted them. "Señorita Carlisle! Should you be here?" he asked in English.

"Mr. Gagehot! What a marvelous stroke of luck. I am looking for Moira. Oh, and this is my escort, Mr. Malvern." Helena turned to Malvern. "This is Papa's British agent for his sherry. He has often visited us in Spain."

"But of course! You are looking for Moira," Gagehot said.

"I have a *carta amorosa* for her from Papa. Is she here?"

Mr. Gagehot did not look happy to hear of this *carta amorosa*. "She was here, but she found it rowdy and mentioned she would leave early. Perhaps she has already gone—"

"Oh, dear! Do you have her address?"

"Let me take the billet-doux to her, to save you bother."

"*Gracias*, but I promised Papa I would deliver it by hand."

A trilling voice screeched across the noisy hall. "Helena! *Cara mía*, it is you!"

"Moira!"

Helena ran to meet a lady wearing an elaborate gown from the reign of Louis XIV, with her reddish blond hair piled in a mound on top of her head. Malvern, ogling her, thought she resembled a slightly passé Rubens. She had that ripe, sensuous quality of his nudes: an expanse of full bosoms, white, dimpled arms, and a pretty but somewhat vacuous face with drooping eyelids. He felt that she would stand no chance of marrying a peer in England, though she stood a very good chance of being kept by one. Something in her suggested an easy availability. She was a trifle tipsy, for one thing.

Helena presented Malvern to her and then suggested, "Let us retire to a quieter corner to talk."

"*Cara mía*, there are no quiet corners to be had here." Mrs. Petrel-Jones laughed. "All is madness and gaiety. I adore it. I could think I am back in Spain. How is your papa?"

Helena drew out the letter. "He wanted me to give you this, Moira. It will explain what he wants to say. May I call on you?"

This struck her as a happier notion than that of asking Moira to call at Belgrave Square. She had grown accustomed to Moira's style in Spain, but in England, her manner seemed somehow unsuitable. Perhaps it was that revealing costume. . . . She felt in her bones that Severn would despise her, and she did not want to subject Papa's friend to a snub.

Moira snatched eagerly at the letter and stuffed it unopened into her bosom. "This is not for your eyes, Lester," she said, with a flirtatious glance at Gagehot.

Once again Helena was smitten with the lady's free manner. Even the word *vulgar* came to mind. Surely she had not behaved like this in the old days? She said nervously, "I really must run along. I am due at a party."

"You *are* at a party, *cara mía*," Mrs. Petrel-Jones said, stiffening up. "Or are your old friends not good

117

enough for you, now that you are moving in higher society?"

"Don't be absurd!" Helena said, chagrined. "My chaperon does not know I am here, so I must leave at once."

"Juan Ortega was speaking to me of you," Moira said. "He hoped to have a word with you tonight. Something about finding him some employment, poor fellow."

"I should like to speak with him," Helena said doubtfully. She was by no means sure this was the time to do it.

"We'll order wine and send someone to find him," Moira said, and led the party to a table. While ordering the wine, she asked the waiter to send Juan to them.

"Well, Mr. Malvern," Mrs. Petrel-Jones said, turning a sharp eye on him, "are you Helena's beau?"

"Mr. Malvern is a friend," Helena said dampingly.

"He's handsome," Moira said, with a coy smile. When the wine arrived, she filled a glass and drank it in one swallow. "It is so hot in here," she scolded, and filled her glass again.

Helena realized the lady had been drinking heavily. That accounted for her manner, so noticeably cruder than it had been in Spain.

Malvern drank his wine up rather quickly, too. "We really should be getting back, Lady Helena."

Moira looked up and said, "Ah, here is Juan. You cannot leave yet. He will be performing a *jota* for us. You always adored the *jota*, Helena."

"Yes, indeed." Juan wore a red satin suit with black braid work on the jacket. A white lace jabot was worn in lieu of a cravat. The rich color and texture suited his dark, Spanish looks. His lithe, young body showed to perfection. He might have been a prince of the royal blood from the last century.

She greeted Juan, then turned to Malvern. "The *jota* is a folk dance of Spain. It is danced by a man and a woman."

"Very romantic." Moira sighed, with another of those coy looks. "You should give your gent a chance to see it, Helena."

"Another time, perhaps," Helena said, rising.

"My, aren't we snobby!" Moira said in a carrying voice. "You didn't stand so high on your dignity in Spain. Many's the time I've seen you perform the *jota* yourself, miss, with all the flirting tricks of a common wench. I told Juan you would partner him."

"I performed it only at Papa's harvest party," Helena reminded her. "This is different."

"Let us ask the party if they would like to see it," Moira said, and rose. In Spanish, she announced that Lady Helena Carlisle, daughter of Lord Aylesbury of the Viñedo Paraíso, was with them. Would they like to see her perform the *jota*? A loud chorus rose, accompanied by glasses thumping on the table.

Lady Helena rose angrily. "Moira, how could you! This is most improper. You know I shouldn't even be here. If Lord Severn found out . . . Let us leave at once, Malvern."

He was happy to escape. He rose immediately and took her arm. But when they tried to leave, a crowd formed around them, hollering, *"Jota, jota, jota."*

Juan smiled apologetically. In Spanish he said,

119

"It will be easiest to oblige the crowd, señorita. I am sorry. Pray do not let this influence you against me."

"I know this is not your doing, Juan."

The music had already begun. Juan took her arm, and the crowd fell back. Someone handed her a red, fringed scarf, and Juan arranged it around her shoulders. They moved to the center of the room. Juan moved back a step and began clapping his hands in time with the beat of the music. The crowd took up the beat, clapping and stamping their feet.

The last conscious thought Helena had was that she was glad Severn was not there to see her make a fool of herself. Then the music seized her, and she began the ritualistic steps of the dance. It was a reenactment of the courting rites, and Juan was a perfect paradigm of Spanish male beauty.

The man entreated and the woman withdrew, not without casting an encouraging flash of eyes over her shoulder. He advanced; she showed disdain by a snap of her fingers and a toss of her curls. For several bars Juan pursued, Helena retreated. Rational thought had left her. The throbbing music dictated what her body would do. For the moments of the dance, she ceased being Lady Helena and became a Spanish girl, hot-blooded, passionate, thinking of nothing but her black-eyed, eager suitor.

The tempo of the music increased, and their feet moved faster. Their eyes were locked now in a battle of wills, giving an undertone of tense passion to the performance. The crowd watched with bated breath as the couple performed the time-honored ritual. The man inched slowly closer, as she first withdrew, then slowly edged closer, until they were within touching distance.

When his hands encircled her waist, she gave him one last, boldly proud look. Then her head lowered a moment, and when it rose again, she was smiling. She writhed temptingly, half encouraging, half disdaining. The end of the crimson shawl was raised to cover her face in a simulation of shyness.

Juan ripped it impatiently from her fingers. The shawl fell to the ground in a silken puddle as the music reached a crescendo. Juan's feet beat a ferocious tattoo as Helena fell perfectly still, overcome by his machismo. His arms reached for her. She glided forward into them, as if mesmerized. His arms closed around her, holding her close now. He tilted her body backward, his head inches from hers. They hung suspended as the music died. Then they rose and exchanged a smile. Juan bowed punctiliously and lifted her hand to his lips.

"Formidable, señorita," he whispered to her. White teeth flashed in his swarthy face, which gleamed with perspiration.

"Gracias, señor."

He lifted her hand in a salute to the crowd, which applauded wildly. Helena performed a few curtsies and looked into the crowd to find Malvern. They must escape before someone demanded an encore. He was not with Moira and Mr. Gagehot, who had moved close to the front of the crowd. Where could he be? Her eyes moved along past the throng hovering at the doorway, then stopped and widened in horror. It couldn't be! It was an illusion, or a nightmare. There, white and rigid with disapproval, was Lord Severn.

Chapter Fourteen

Helena's first instinct was to flee, but Severn was already advancing, stiff-legged, but making very good time. She stood motionless as a trapped rabbit, unable to move for the wild beating of her heart. He took her arm in a firm grip and led her away without a word. How had he found her? How had he known where to come so quickly?

It had not seemed so quick to Severn. He suspected nothing amiss until he stood up with Marion. It was she who said, "Mr. Malvern is a wonderful dancer. I was sorry it was only a country dance we shared." Her intention was not to harm Helena, but to alert Severn that he had competition for her own hand.

"Is *he* here?" Severn grumbled.

"Yes, standing up with Helena, I expect." They glanced around the floor. Within minutes, they knew that Malvern had disappeared. Marion was sent up to the ladies' room and discovered Helena's absence. A query to the butler told them neither party had left, not by the front door, at least.

"I can soon tell you if Mr. Malvern is gone, your lordship, for he had a case put away that he meant to take with him when he left," the butler told them.

He led them to the small parlor, where they discovered that the case was gone. As the side door had been left ajar in their haste, it was not long before the worst was suspected.

"A bolt for the border, by God," Severn said in a hollow voice. He was too shocked to be angry yet.

Marion would not hear of such a thing. "Impossible. Mr. Malvern is calling on me tomorrow afternoon. *She* has talked him into some folly. You may be sure it has to do with her precious Spaniards. There were posters at El Cafeto advertising a ball. A *baile mascarado*, or something of the sort. The picture showed a masked couple. Perhaps it is being held tonight."

Severn listened closely. "That would explain Malvern's case—a change of outfits. She arranged this behind my back."

"She would hardly expect *you* to connive at it," Marion pointed out. There was disapproval in her tone, though he had expected complete support. "We had best go after them, Severn."

"No need for you to come. I shall bring her back."

"But you don't know where El Cafeto is."

"On Orange Street, off Haymarket, I believe."

"How did you know that?" she asked.

"Don't mention to your mama or anyone that she is gone" was Severn's reply. "I'll have her back before she is missed."

"Be sure you bring Malvern back, too," Marion said, with a faintly ironic smile. "I shall ring a peal over him."

Severn suffered a few pangs as he rattled along toward Orange Street. What if he was wrong? What

123

if she *had* darted to Gretna Green with Malvern? That case the fellow was carrying looked bad. But Helena had carried no case. She would not leave without her beautiful gowns. In his mind, it was not her white deb's gowns he envisaged, but the flamboyant colors of her first days.

Perhaps he had been too severe on her for that visit to El Cafeto. If he had not made so much of it, she might have asked him to take her to this masquerade ball. Naturally she was lonesome for something familiar to her. There could be no harm in a Spanish ball. She had assured him propriety was strictly enforced in Spain. Except that Malvern was hardly a proper *dueña*. He gave the drawstring two sharp jerks to encourage his driver to go faster.

As he entered the somewhat dilapidated Orange Street and saw the revelers weaving along, drunk as lords, half of them, he feared this *baile mascarado* was no polite affair. The hand-painted sign directed him to the proper doorway. He leapt out and told John Groom to keep the carriage standing by. As he took the stairs two at a time, he had some reviving hope that the party was not totally abandoned. The only sound was the swirling Spanish music, with an underbeat of clapping. There was no drunken brawling or coarse shouting, at least.

When he paid his admission and entered the hall, he saw the crowd around the edge of the room and realized some performance was going forth—dancers performing to the music. He looked around the throng. They ignored him completely; every eye was on the performers. He continued on his way, wondering what sort of outfits Helena and Malvern were wearing. Simple dominoes and masks, very likely. At least no one would recognize her.

As he passed behind a clutch of seated older ladies, he was able to get a glimpse of the performance. Juan's red suit, trimmed with black, caught
his eye first. A fine figure of a man, but it was the
lady in white who lent fire to the performance. Her
back was to Severn, and he saw first her sinuous
body, with arms raised gracefully. He watched, entranced, as she shifted away from the pursuing
Juan. His heart beat faster as Juan masterfully
overcame the woman's scruples and she surren-
dered herself to him with supple compliance. The
theme of the dance was easily comprehensible. As
Juan drew the woman, unresisting now, into his
arms and lowered her to the floor, something stirred
deep within Severn.

One could not say the dance was obscene, for it
was done with exquisite grace and skill, but it was
certainly erotic. Really, it hardly seemed a proper
performance for mixed company. He disliked to
think of Helena watching it. Actually, the danseuse
looked a little like her. He gazed on as Juan lifted
the dancer back on her feet and they both made
their bows. Really, she looked remarkably like—*no!*
It *couldn't* be. She wouldn't dare! But it was she.
His heart slowed to a heavy thud; his hands
bunched to fists and he edged past the seated ladies
on to the floor.

Helena was gasping from the dance and from an
unpleasant combination of anger and fear. As he
seized her wrist and led her to the door, she managed to gasp, "My reticule."

"Where is it?"

"There." She pointed to the table, to which Gagehot and Moira were just returning. Thank God
Malvern was not with them. He must have slipped

away when he recognized Severn. Severn glared at Gagehot and Moira. "I'll get it," Helena said, for she didn't want to present Severn to Moira in her present state.

Gagehot, still sober and respectable, rose and said, "Good evening" to Severn, whose only reply was a filthy glare.

"This is my father's wine agent, Mr. Gagehot," Helena said. "And Mrs. Petrel-Jones," she added perforce. "May I present Lord Severn."

Severn did not bow, offer his hand, or even say, "Good evening." "We must leave at once," he said in icy accents. Then he snatched up Helena's reticule and handed it to her.

"And my domino," she said. While retrieving it from the chair, she managed to draw a few sovereigns out of her wallet, to allow Mr. Malvern to hire a cab home. She left them on the seat, hoping he would find them.

"Come along," Severn said impatiently, and reached for the domino. Its tail caught the coins. They flew to the floor, rattling under the table, but not before Severn had seen them. "An odd place to leave a pourboire," he said, arching a hateful eyebrow at her.

"A Spanish custom," she replied, and left with a nod to her former companions. A path opened to allow the angry milord to lead his friend away.

As Severn marched her down the stairs and out to the carriage, he didn't trust himself to speak. He felt betrayed, as if he had found her working in a brothel. "Take us home," he called to his groom, and shoved her onto the banquette.

Helena, too, was silent, planning her explanation. When they had gone a block and still Severn did not speak, she screwed up her courage for the verbal confrontation. "It was not what you think, Severn," she said.

"I trust it was not, for I could hardly give you permission to marry a Spanish dancer. Nothing short of a betrothal could explain that performance, and even *that* would not excuse it. Women usually conduct such affairs in private. Unmarried ladies, I need hardly say, do not conduct such affairs at all."

"It was only a dance. It is a common practice in Spain."

"It is exceedingly 'common' in England, madam. Worse than common! I have never seen such an indecent performance."

"It was not indecent! The *jota* is beautiful. It is only your lecherous English mind that imputes any immorality to it. I have often performed the *jota* at Papa's harvest festivals."

"What degree of latitude you were allowed in Spain has nothing to do with it. You are in England now, masquerading as a lady. While you are under my roof, you will behave with some shred, at least, of propriety. Every door in town would be barred to you if anyone had the least suspicion of this night's work. Good God! You might as well hire yourself out and go on the stage. At least you would be paid for making a public spectacle of yourself. Sneaking off behind my back, lying to me!"

"I did not lie!" she retorted. "And if you were more *simpático*, I would not have to sneak off behind your back."

The grain of truth in her charge only increased his wrath. "You lied by omission. You knew I would

127

not permit you to go there. I shall call Malvern out for this."

"Malvern?" she exclaimed. "What makes you think he had anything to do with it?"

"I am not a fool. Don't bother trying to shield him."

"It is not Malvern's fault, Eduardo," she said, clutching his arm. "I made him take me. He said it was wrong of me."

"Then he should not have abetted you. What wiles did you use to persuade him?"

"I did not use wiles. I explained my need, and he, having a heart, agreed to accompany me, for he knew I would go alone if he did not. And if you dare to call him out—"

He turned an icy eye on her. "Like that, is it? You have an unerring eye for a bad bargain. I can well believe you brought the poor fool round your finger. It would be cruel to shoot him for his idiocy, but that does not mean he will be given permission to marry your fortune."

Helena sank against the squabs of the carriage, suddenly exhausted. She put her fingers to her throbbing temples and said weakly, "Thank God this night is over."

Severn had been too upset to think straight, but her words brought him back to sanity. It had been his plan to return her to Mrs. Stephen's rout, hoping to avoid suspicion that she had ever left. "It is not over. We shall return to Mrs. Stephen's rout," he said, but the carriage sped toward Belgrave Square.

When his hand reached for the cord, she said, "Oh, please, Eduardo. I could not face it. Can we not go home?"

His hand held motionless, halfway to the draw

128

cord. "It will be best if you return to the rout. People will be wondering at your absence."

"Could you not go back and say you had to take me home?" she asked in a small voice. "You could say I had a megrim. It would not be a lie, for my poor head is splitting."

A weakening stab of pity warred with his anger. "Why did you do it?" he demanded harshly.

Her head dropped on her chest. "I had to go," she said.

"Had you arranged to perform at that ball?"

She sprang up straight. "No! Good gracious, I didn't want to do it. I was forced into it. Moira announced that I was there and that I would do the *jota*. It is an old and favorite folk dance of the country, performed at all their festivals. The crowd gathered around me and would not let me escape. Juan—that was the man I danced with—said it would be easier to just do the dance, then I could leave."

"Juan is the fellow you plan to have play at your ball?"

"Yes, but only to play the guitar and perhaps sing. I did not plan to foist the *jota* onto Englishmen."

The name Moira, of course, rang a bell. Severn said, "This Moira you spoke of, was she the vulgar hussy at your table?"

"Yes, she is a friend of Papa's. I had to deliver her a letter. That is why I went to the masquerade. I learned at El Cafeto today that she would be there. I went to El Cafeto only to look for her. I am sorry if you think it was horrid of me, but what could I do? I promised Papa I would deliver his letter, Eduardo," she said in a wheedling way.

When she looked at him with her big dark eyes and her lips drawn into an adorable moue, Severn had an inkling he was being manipulated. He found it quite delightful to be managed by a beautiful, clever lady. And, really, her story was by no means incredible. It could have happened just as she said. Indeed he could hardly imagine any other way it could have come about.

"You should have told me, Cousin," he said, and drew her small white hand into his. "I am not quite the monster you take me for, you know. I daresay if I had been there, you would not have been forced into that dance."

Her head subsided onto his shoulder. "Indeed no. You would have protected me. You won't make me go back to Mrs. Stephen's, Eduardo? My head really does ache. I have a wretched throbbing, as if drums were beating inside it."

"I'll take you home," he said. Then he lifted one hand and drew it slowly across her temple.

"That feels good." She sighed, closing her eyes. She could hardly believe she had soothed Severn's savage temper so easily. How angry he had been! Almost more angry than the occasion demanded—unless there was a little jealousy mixed in with it? His fingers continued to work at her temple, drawing slowly from the front, back into her hair, in a slow, soothing way. Gradually the backward stroke lengthened, until his fingers were coiled in her silken curls.

She turned her face and smiled up at him in the shadowy carriage. "What are you doing, Eduardo?" Her face was a pale heart, with a gleam of dark eyes and a flash of white teeth.

He watched a moment, entranced; then his head lowered and his lips touched her eyes. "Trying to ease your migraine," he said. His voice sounded husky.

She continued gazing at him while her lips formed a soft smile. "It feels good. Don't stop."

A warm breath fanned his cheek. At this close range, he noticed some exotic perfume escaping from her curls. He remembered her dance and felt that tingling excitement stir again within him. "Helena, darling . . ." His lips seized hers, and when she did not pull away, they firmed for a kiss.

It was madness, an intoxicating delirium of desire burning deep within him. His arms went around her and crushed her against his chest. Nothing else in the world mattered but this woman, who yielded herself softly to him. The carriage drew to a stop. When he opened his eyes, he saw they were home.

Helena drew back and smiled. "That was rather naughty of you, Eduardo," she said, shaking a finger at him. He looked so chagrined that she laughed. "And very nice," she added, placing a quick kiss on his cheek.

"I'll take you in, then return to the rout and explain you were not feeling well. How is the headache?" he asked gently.

"Much better. You are more *simpático* than I thought, Cousin. I am sorry I have been such a nuisance to you."

"Nuisances have their reward," he said, smiling. "The letter to Moira is delivered now. You won't have to see her again. I don't know what your father is about, encouraging that creature. Let us hope the letter is giving her her congé."

Helena did not wish to be any further nuisance that evening, and she left him with his delusions. He accompanied her to the door, then returned to the carriage and to the rout to make her excuses. Malvern, he noticed, had not returned. He gave an expurgated version of the incident to Marion, omitting any mention of the *jota*. As he and Marion had not had their dance earlier, he stood up with her to keep her in spirits.

Lady Hadley's guests were having a late supper when Lady Helena went inside. She just explained that she had left the party early due to a headache, said, "Good evening," and went upstairs. Sally noticed her ladyship was very quiet that evening as she prepared for bed.

Helena had a lot to think about. Severn, clearly, was falling in love with her. That should have been gratifying, as he would be putty in her hands from now on. But somehow, it was not satisfying. She did not want to hurt him, for he was really much nicer than she had thought. If only he were not such a stiff and proper *inglés*, she might even contrive to fall in love with him.

But with unfinished business to conduct with Moira, she did not feel he would continue so *simpático* as he had been that evening. He did not want her to see "that creature" again. What would he say when he learned she called on Moira again? She must do so. She had agreed to it, and, besides, Papa loved her. What would Severn do if Papa married Moira? He would not want to be connected to such a person. She hardly relished the idea herself. Either Moira had changed or she had changed herself, become nicer in her notions of propriety. More English. Oh, dear, life was difficult.

Chapter Fifteen

The next morning at breakfast, Severn was in high spirits. As Lady Hadley was still in bed after her late night, he had privacy with Lady Helena. "Marion mentioned calling on you this morning, Cousin," he said. "I daresay you ladies will be plundering the shops on New Bond Street."

"Is she coming in the morning or afternoon?" Helena asked.

"Early afternoon. Of course, you will take a groom, if neither Mama nor Mrs. Comstock wishes to accompany you."

"I always take a groom, Eduardo. You do not have to remind me of the proprieties. Well, hardly ever," she added, with a secret smile over the coffee cup. Cook had been instructed to serve Lady Helena coffee in the morning.

Severn answered her smile. He wished the footman would leave so that they might have a more interesting conversation. "Perhaps you would like to come with me to Westminster this morning to hear me speak?"

"I would like it, of all things," she said, "but I have to write to Papa. You know—about last night."

"Best to get that out of the way. I shan't be late

today. If you and Marion can be home by four, you and I could take a spin through Hyde Park."

"I shall try," she said.

Before leaving, Severn said, "No need to mention last night's affair to Mama, Helena. It will be our secret." He smiled warmly and left.

Helena sat on, thinking. In the uproar of last night's doings, she had somehow forgotten to discover Moira's address. She wanted to visit her that morning. Perhaps Gagehot could tell her. He usually stayed at Reddishes Hotel when he was in London. She went to the desk in the saloon to dash off a note. Halfway through it, Sugden entered.

"A note has come for you, milady," he said, handing her a folded sheet of paper. "The footman is waiting for an answer."

"Thank you." She skimmed the note. It was from Moira, bearing belabored apologies for last night, with much underlining and many exclamation points. She did not know what Lady Helena must think of her. She had not been herself, but ever since her altercation with dear Algernon, she had been so very unhappy, etc., etc. It ended with a request that Helena come to her apartment on Upper Grosvenor Square as soon as possible.

Lady Helena said, "No written reply is necessary, Sugden. Tell the footman I shall be happy to do as requested. And would you have my carriage sent around, please? I shall require the escort of a groom. You can tell Lady Hadley I have gone out but shall be home for lunch."

"Yes, your ladyship." Sugden bowed and left.

Well, that was arranged very neatly. She dressed for outdoors at once, and when she came downstairs, her carriage was waiting. The visit held no pleasure for her, except the possibility of making her father happy. She must try to hint Moira away from overindulging in wine.

Helena knew as soon as she entered the building that Moira was living in a lower style than she had done in Spain. Had Papa provided that lavish hacienda for her? Her present apartment was on the third floor, and when Helena reached the door, she noticed the hallway was dusty. Moira had a servant to answer the door, however, and show the caller into a small parlor. The chamber could not be called a saloon, for it lacked both size and grandeur.

Moira lacked neither. Her hair was arranged in an intricate do more suited to a ball. It lacked only a clutch of feathers. She had fallen into flesh. Her bright blue gown with many bows and a surfeit of lace strained at the seams. In the clear light of day, the signs of dissipation were easily seen. Purple puffs bulged below her eyes, and her cheeks sagged with weight. Moira had always appreciated Papa's fine sherry, but Helena had thought it was consumed to flatter her father.

"Dear child, you came!" Moira said, holding out her hand but not rising from the chair. Helena went to her to exchange an embrace. Fumes of sherry enveloped the woman. "I was touched to receive Algernon's *carta amorosa*. He still wants me, dear."

"I am happy for you, Moira. Then you will write and tell him you accept?"

Moira wagged a roguish finger. "I have not quite made up my mind. Certain details are still to be worked out. I shall insist on a certain allowance and, of course, my own carriage."

This sounded more like the demands of a mistress than those of a wife, but Helena held her

135

tongue. "Your papa has a little competition now," Moira said, with a sly look. "And returning to Spain ... Well, it is so hot there, I am used to England now."

"Papa will never come to England. Not to live, I mean. Perhaps he will agree to visit from time to time."

"He'll come home if he wants me. And he does. You ought to read his letter." She offered Helena a glass of sherry. When she declined, Moira filled her own glass and drank deeply.

"You will write him of your demands?" And I shall write to warn him what state you are in, Helena added to herself.

"You may be sure of it. So how do you like it with your relatives, dear? That Severn seems a pretty toplofty number." Her speech became less elevated as she drank.

"I am having a nice time. Only of course, I miss Spain."

"Sly rogue!" Moira laughed. "You say so only to convince me to join your papa."

"About Papa's competition, Moira ... Who is the man?"

"That would be telling," Moira said archly, and drank some more sherry. "But I'll let you in on this much, and I don't mind if you tell your father either. Gagehot has done pretty well for himself with some investments. He does not want to go back to Spain. He doesn't see why he could not handle your father's business from London."

"I see." Gagehot was a far step down from Lord Aylesbury, but if Moira had him in her eye, Helena would not say a word against it. "He is very handsome," she said.

"Handsome doesn't begin to say it. He knows how to treat a lady. Look at this," she said, holding out a pudgy hand to display a large pearl ring.

"Magnificent." Taking jewelry from another man! Really, the woman was little better than a lightskirt.

"Tell *that* to your father," Moira said complacently. She glanced at her watch. "Look at the time! Lester will be here any moment. I must have some coffee." She rose from her chair on unsteady legs and called her servant. It would take more than coffee to sober her up if Gagehot was to arrive within the next hour.

"I'll be running along now. It was nice to see you again."

"Don't be a stranger, dear. I never blamed you for what your papa said to me."

Helena stopped in her tracks. "What did he say?"

"You don't think I turned him off for no reason? He told me I was too fond of the bottle. Fancy that, right to my face. I told him I wasn't about to sit still for that. I upped and left. I knew he'd call me back, and so he has. Now that I'm a widow, he wants to marry me."

Helena's eyes slid to the wine decanter on the side table. "I don't remember ever seeing you . . . tipsy . . . in Spain."

Moira slumped back onto her chair. "Oh, it's gotten worse, dear. It has. I came home determined to lay off the wine, for it was being in such high company that I wasn't used to that caused it. But here in England I was that lonesome. You've no idea. Then two weeks ago Gagehot returned. . . ." She smiled fondly. "And now *he's* ripping up at me."

"Oh, Moira," Helena said, torn between exasper-

137

ation and pity. "You're going to lose both of them, carrying on like this. Can't you stop?"

"It's not for lack of trying, dear. My father was taken the same way. But I will try. I will. It was the high company—my nerves needed a little sustaining. I wager it'll happen again if I go back to Algernon."

"Perhaps you'd be happier with Gagehot," Helena suggested.

Moira bristled up. "Easy for you to say. You've already got one title and will soon have another, I don't doubt. Severn acted as if he owned you. They're all alike, the fine lords. Wouldn't your Severn look down his needle nose at me!"

The servant came with the coffee, and Helena used it as an excuse to leave. She went straight home and wrote her father a note describing her visit. "If you love her, Papa, insist she stop drinking before you marry her. If she loves you, she will do it. And if you love her, you should recall Gagehot to Spain, not that he will necessarily heed your summons. I am having a lovely Season. I miss you. Your loving daughter, Helena."

Over lunch, she told Lady Hadley of her morning visit and felt better for having someone older to advise her.

"Mercy! She sounds horrid. Algernon always had low taste in women. I do not mean your mama, my dear. I never met her. But before he left England, he always had some unseemly bit o' muslin in tow. He would not be thinking of marrying this Petrel person if there were any decent English ladies there."

"I think you are right, *Madrina*. I met very few English ladies and did not realize Moira was so vulgar. Her husband was an officer, you know; she followed the drum a few years with him. That would be bound to have a lowering effect. When she behaved differently from our other friends, I thought it was just the English way. Now that I have met many *inglesas*, I see she is different. I hope she marries Mr. Gagehot. Papa will find a new flirt and get over her."

"Could we help Gagehot along, do you think?"

"Perhaps Papa could give him a better-paying post in London, with no need to go to Spain. Moira doesn't want to go back. I fear it would be fatal to her health and happiness—to say nothing of Papa's—if she did."

Helena began remembering the better days with Moira and wished she could help her. She must help her; it was a lady's duty. She said, "Whatever else we do or do not accomplish, *Madrina*, I must help Moira overcome this love of sherry. She acquired her fondness for it when she was with Papa, so in a way it is his fault. He would do no less if he were here."

"I believe there are nursing homes that treat such cases."

"She would never enter one voluntarily, and I have no authority to have her committed. I must visit her again soon. With Gagehot's help, I might exert some slight influence."

"But if she recovers, there is no saying Algernon won't marry her. I cannot like to see him make a fool of himself again. As if marrying a Sp—" She came to an embarrassed stop. "Well, if he does marry her, at least she will be sober."

"And English," Helena added, with a quizzing smile.

"It just slipped out. If your mama was anything like you, I am sure Algernon was more fortunate than he deserved."

"I am not offended, *Madrina*. Friends may be quite truthful with each other without giving offense. I wish I could achieve such a frank arrangement with Severn. You and I can speak to each other without coming to cuffs. One would think a young man would be more lenient than his mama in social matters."

"I see my son has been nagging at you. He is becoming like his papa since he began visiting Whitehall. We shan't mention your little scheme to him."

Helena went abovestairs to prepare for lunch. She hoped she could keep straight in her head just what was a secret from whom.

Chapter Sixteen

Marion came alone for the carriage drive that afternoon. Her mama was entertaining some friends at tea. Marion wore a dashing new bonnet and a new coiffure. She did not look lovely; nature is not that easily influenced. But she looked better. Her manner was also less disagreeable than formerly. She complimented Helena on her bonnet and smiled twice during a brief conversation with Lady Hadley.

"Let us go to Hyde Park today," she said when they went out to the tilbury. "We have been to Bond Street so often."

"It is a little early. The crowd won't be there yet."

"We could descend and go for a walk. It's a lovely day."

It sounded a dull scald to Helena, but the driving was easier, and she welcomed the opportunity for some quiet thinking. They went to Hyde Park, where Lady Helena handed the reins to her groom while she and Marion enjoyed a quiet stroll along one of the paths. Before they had walked fifty yards, Mr. Malvern detached himself from a tree and came toward them.

Helena's instinct was to run back to the carriage. She owed Mr. Malvern an apology and would make it, but not when Marion was present, with her ears on the stretch. She said, "Let us go back to the carriage, Marion."

Marion gave her a cool look. "Because of Mr. Malvern? I should think you would welcome the chance to apologize to him. Oh yes, I know all about last night. Malvern told me."

"I see. In that case, I shall make my apology, and then we shall leave."

Malvern advanced uncertainly, watching their faces for a clue to his likely welcome.

"Mr. Malvern, what a surprise," Marion said. She was so unaccustomed to prevarication that a child could see she had planned the meeting.

"I am dreadfully sorry for last night," Helena said. "Leaving without even saying good-bye or thanking you. Did you ... er ... manage to get home all right?" She did not like to mention the money in front of Marion.

"Certainly I did. I am grateful to see that you survived. Severn looked ready to kill someone, and as you were kind enough not to lead him in my direction, I feared you might be the casualty. I returned to Stephen's after he had left."

"I managed to tame the savage beast, but I fear he knew somehow that you were my accomplice." She smiled.

"That is my fault," Marion said. "I let it slip last night. I saw the two of you heading for the door together. If you had taken me into your confidence, I might have helped you."

Helena stared at her cousin as if she had run mad. Ask Marion's help in chicanery? She would as soon ask the pope to swear. "Somehow that did not occur to me," she said blankly. She noticed from

142

the corner of her eye that Marion had linked her arm through Malvern's.

Marion said, "Let us continue our stroll, Cousin." Then she turned to Malvern and directed her conversation to him.

The words "last evening" were often repeated. Soon Helena figured out that Malvern had returned to Mrs. Stephen's rout and told Marion the whole story. She assumed it was then that this assignation had been set up. They were using her and her carriage as a means of carrying out this clandestine meeting!

She might be in Malvern's debt, but she owed Marion nothing. Her hot blood rose and she said, "I really must be going now. It was nice meeting you again, Mr. Malvern."

"I hope we shall meet again soon, and often, Lady Helena." Then he bowed punctiliously and left.

Helena turned a wrathful eye on Marion. "You arranged this meeting, Marion, and don't bother to deny it."

Marion tossed her head. "What of it? You have done worse. You convinced Malvern to take you to that masquerade ball."

"I see you are his confidante! I had a very good reason for requiring his escort to that ball, and I did not involve you in it. You have involved me in your little escapade."

Marion jumped to his defense. "Ladies are always using him! They think because he has no fortune that he may be sent hither and thither, doing things they would not ask someone they consider worthier to do. Malvern is a gentleman, and if you have further need of an escort to undesirable places,

143

I would appreciate your asking someone else to accompany you."

"You sound extremely proprietary, Marion. What is it to you if Malvern helps me from time to time? Your mama would never allow you to marry him. I would not have thought an *à suivi* flirtation just in your style?" Her cool inflection made it a question.

Marion looked her in the eye and replied boldly, "Perhaps you don't know me as well as you think. As to Malvern's eligibility, he has breeding, if not money. Between us, we could manage. He is very clever, you must know."

"I see you have been giving this a deal of thought. If I were in your shoes, I would ask myself whether it was me or my money he is interested in."

"I would ask myself the same thing if I were you, being courted by Severn," Marion retorted.

"I am not being courted by Severn! And he has plenty of blunt of his own."

"He hasn't that much while Lord Hadley is alive, and the Hadleys are long livers. He would like to have twenty-five thousand at his beck and call."

They walked toward the carriage in silence after that frank exchange. It was the second time someone had hinted to Helena that it was her fortune Severn was interested in. Malvern had said the same thing last night.

When the groom was driving them home, Helena said, "I don't see that Severn has any need of my money. He lives in a very good style. He doesn't gamble, or keep a lightskirt, or have any expensive vices so far as I have determined." Marion snorted. "Well, has he?"

"Not at the moment," Marion said.

"He must have some money of his own to cover his daily expenses. An allowance, or inheritance."

"He is actually quite well to grass, but he does have one expensive vice." Helena's eyes widened in interest. "His new vice appears to be politics. The parties are always looking for money to buy rotten boroughs or advance their various causes. The court sinecures mostly go to the Tories, since Prinny has taken up with Lady Hertford. I have often heard Brougham bemoan the Whigs' lack of funds. If Severn contributed heavily to the party coffers, there would be some onus on Brougham to repay him with a top position if they ever come into power."

"Good God," Helena murmured. "I thought the wine business was corrupt, but it is nothing compared to this. And Severn speaking as if he were Caesar's wife, lecturing me for any little thing."

Marion gave a sardonic smile. "Perhaps he is training you up to be his wife. The Whigs are known for their clever hostesses. You wanted a great man, Helena. A great man requires a wife who behaves with propriety, as well as having a fortune. You notice the duke hasn't called on you recently."

"What do you mean?" Helena asked at once.

"I daresay Severn hinted him away."

The carriage jogged on. The ladies sat, not glaring at each other, but not enjoying a comfortable silence either. The air bristled with animosity.

Marion was to be delivered to her own house that day, as Mrs. Comstock was receiving company. Lady Helena was invited in, but she declined and returned to Belgrave Square.

Her mind was awhirl with the ideas Marion had planted in it. Severn courting her for her fortune?

Severn training her up for a proper political hostess? Severn turning Rutledge off? It was not to be borne. Secret knowledge was power. She would not confront him with her knowledge, but she would bear it in mind. A lady's inferior social position required her to employ more guile, and in all modesty, she felt she outstripped Severn in that respect.

She was all amiability when he returned early from the House. "Did you and Marion have a nice drive?" he asked.

"Lovely. We went to Hyde Park at an early hour to avoid the crowds." She said not a word about meeting Malvern. "Marion invited me to her place for tea, but I knew you would be home early," she said, modestly lowering her lashes.

Severn accepted this as his due. "I made a special effort to get away early. Brougham was not too pleased with me, I fear. He had called a meeting about raising the wind to help out a young fellow we got elected in a by-election. The fellow is a fine orator, but his pockets are to let."

"Could some paying position not be found for him?" she asked innocently.

"That is not so easy for us Whigs to arrange, but Oxford is putting in a word with some friends of his."

"It must be hard to run a party that is not in power. People are more likely to contribute to the reigning party, in hopes of receiving some political reward."

"You have hit the nail on the head, Helena. You have a good grasp of politics. You would make a fine political hostess," he added, taking her hand and gazing into her eyes.

Was this his idea of courting? She was furious.

She hoped her angry flush might be mistaken for a blush and made a simpering face. They did not go out for a drive after all.

Severn delivered a lecture on politics instead, and Helena pretended to hang on his every word. Since their embrace in the carriage, he was beginning to think marrying her would not be such an imposition, and it would please Papa.

At the ball that evening, Helena made sure to stand up with Rutledge and behaved with the maximum allowable degree of flirtation. When he did not ask if he might call the next day, she felt Marion was right. Severn had hinted him away. Her fury rose a notch.

The next morning and for the next few subsequent days, she went to call on Mrs. Petrel-Jones, always informing her that she would return the next morning, in hopes that this would at least delay the day's drinking. She bought pamphlets on the evil of drink from a street stall and gave them to Moira.

"Please don't think it encroaching of me," she said when she presented them, "but I cannot like to see you like this. You are destroying your health. And your looks, Moira," she added daringly. Being a lady herself, Helena knew this warning might have more weight than the rest of the arguments put together.

"It becomes a habit," Moira tried to explain. "When I'm alone, remembering how I thought the world would be when I was young and seeing how it turned out, I just get so melancholy, the only comfort is in the bottle."

"There are places you can go to be cured."

"Lord, they cost the moon!"

"I would be happy to pay, if that is all—"

"I'll not have it said I'm that far gone. I'll *try*, dear. Between you and Lester, you just might cure me yet."

Something seemed to be having some effect. When Helena called on the fourth morning, Moira sat sipping tea. She was completely sober. The customary decanter and glass were not on the table beside her.

"Lester is taking me to meet his sister today," Moira announced. "Now I don't want you thinking it means anything, Helena. It doesn't mean I love your papa a jot less. It is just that Lester is here, and Algernon is an ocean away."

"Of course, I understand. I am sure Papa would like to be here, but you know his work keeps him in Spain."

"Do you think he'll ever come back?"

"Perhaps, for a short visit after the war."

"A short visit," Moira said glumly.

"As you are expecting Gagehot soon, I shall leave early today. I hope you have a nice visit with his sister."

When Helena left the apartment, she waited outside in her tilbury until Gagehot arrived, and she called him to her. He looked as guilty as a poacher with a jiggling bag over his shoulder.

"Will you join me for a moment, Gagehot?" she said.

He got into the carriage. "I daresay you are wondering what brings me here on a work day. Moira is lonesome, poor soul," he said. "I drop in to try to cheer her up."

"That is kind of you, Mr. Gagehot. I wonder if Papa appreciates all you do for him."

He gave her a leery look, suspecting a sting in the tail of that compliment. "I don't neglect your father's business, if that is what—"

"No, no. You misunderstand me. I have noticed several shops selling our sherry," she said, not quite truthfully. "It must take a deal of effort on your part to make so many calls, encouraging buyers."

"That it does," he said, happy to quit the other subject.

"When you are in Spain, who handles the selling to the wholesalers here in England?"

"No one. I do that when I am in England. I spend only a few months in Spain, mostly rounding up continental customers."

"I shall tell Papa you require an assistant, Mr. Gagehot."

His face turned red with annoyance. "If you are suggesting that I ought to spend more time in Spain, Lady Helena, I should tell you that I am reaching that age when I would prefer to be at home more. If he cannot win Mrs. Petrel-Jones by fair—"

"You misunderstand me, sir," she said, directing a speaking glance at him. "I think Papa needs a full-time man in Spain to handle the continental customers, which would allow you to remain in England. You would be in charge of this junior man, with, of course, an increase in salary."

He seemed perplexed at the idea of receiving more money for less work. "Eh?"

"You would make Moira an admirable husband," she said bluntly.

"Not so high and mighty a one as your papa," he said, confused. "Why are you scheming behind your own papa's back to defeat him?" Gagehot demanded.

"Papa has no heir, you know. The family feels a younger lady—"

"Ah, so that's how it is. I shouldn't have thought Moira is past it, but there's no denying she's been fruitless so far. Perhaps it's the drink. I'm trying to curb that unfortunate tendency."

"With some success, too. I believe if she was happily married, with a husband and friends and relatives, she would settle down. She mentioned meeting your sister today."

"I thought that a happy notion myself. Lucy is a great one for running around to the shops and picnics and dances."

"Let me know how it goes. And about that promotion and salary increase, Mr. Gagehot—I shall write to Papa today."

"He won't go for it if he tumbles to your game, milady."

"My game?" she asked innocently. "I only want to see you properly reimbursed for your duties and to cut down on your traveling, now that you have developed that little health problem."

"What problem is that?" he asked, grinning.

"Oh, heart trouble, I think. I shall let you go to her now. Nice talking to you."

"Very nice indeed, Lady Helena." He got out and bowed before turning to the apartment house.

Lady Helena went straight home and wrote to her father, explaining that Mr. Gagehot was worked to the bone and needed an assistant. He really should not be traveling abroad with his troublesome heart.

She received her first letter from her father the next morning, asking if she had found Moira. He sounded so eager that she almost regretted her scheme. In order to break the bad news to him gently, she wrote that she visited Moira daily and was concerned for her health. A return to Spain's harsh climate, she feared, might be fatal. Would it be possible for Papa to live in England?

She had no real fear that he would consider this. He was one of those people who was born in the wrong place. He had felt at home from the moment he first visited Spain. The making of sherry was in his veins. He loved to walk his vineyards, looking at his grapes, tasting them. He spent hours in his winery, blending, testing, laughing, and joking with his workers in fluent Spanish, yet he could not master French after years of lessons. Latin and Greek were a mystery to him as well.

Helena had enjoyed that earlier life, too, but after only a few weeks in England, she found herself liking it very much. Spain would always have a special place in her heart. She would like to take her husband and children there to visit one day. She fell into a reverie of remembering, and daydreaming of the future. After fifteen minutes, she was interrupted by Sally and was amazed to discover that it was Severn who had been strolling the vineyards with her. It was small replicas of him who had been pulling the grapes from the vine and eating them.

"What is it, Sally?" she asked.

"Cook says I can't have no more lemons. I made the terrible mistake of telling Sukey, Cook's helper, what we're doing with them, and she went and told Cook. Just when the juice was beginning to work, too. My spots haven't faded, but my hair's getting so blond, you'd hardly take me for a redhead."

"It looks very nice," Helena said. The red was

beginning to lighten to blond. She didn't want to come to cuffs with *Madrina*'s cook and gave Sally money to buy her own lemons.

Such pettiness, to begrudge the poor girl a lemon a day. They rotted on the ground in Spain. Everything came down to money in England. Moira would have Gagehot if he could keep her in a higher style. Malvern would be considered eligible if his pockets were not to let. And Severn hoped to marry her own fortune, to give it to his beloved Whigs.

Chapter Seventeen

Helena almost felt she was visiting a different lady when she called on Moira the next morning. Moira was bright-eyed and lively, as she used to be in Spain. She served tea, a civility she had forgotten on former visits. Her talk was all of Mrs. Everett, which was Lucy Gagehot's married name.

"Mrs. Everett is very genteel," she said, nodding her head approvingly. "She has her own carriage and all. Well, her husband has, but as he is in his shop all day, she has the use of it. Mr. Everett owns a drapery shop. It is doing a thriving business. He does not stand behind the counter, of course. He sits in his office attending to business. Mrs. Everett and I plan to drop in to see him this morning." She looked at the head-and-shoulders clock on the mantel.

After a few such hints, Helena left, much encouraged. On the second visit after the advent of Mrs. Everett into her life, Moira was calling her new friend "Lucy." She said casually to Helena before she left, "I may not be in tomorrow, so if it is inconvenient for you to call, don't feel obliged. Lucy is having her coiffeur in to do our heads. We are going to Vauxhall Gardens in the evening. You need not mention all this to your papa," she added, but with little concern.

The visits petered out to two a week. Moira was as good as cured. She had found a milieu where she was comfortable without the crutch of alcohol. Helena felt that as soon as Gagehot received his promotion, the wedding would occur.

Helena's own social life proceeded satisfactorily. The duke, encouraged by her new interest, resumed his calls. He seldom had the opportunity to get her to himself, however. She had acquired her own court and was enjoying her success.

Severn was being drawn ever deeper into politics. So long as her callers came in droves, he did not object. There was safety in numbers. Marion still called, but less frequently. Her talk was as often as not of Malvern, who was finding favor with Mrs. Comstock. An experienced courter, he knew the good an infatuated mama could do him and was lavish with his compliments, assistance in fetching and carrying, and was always available for those difficulties that troubled a manless home.

Beaufort had been approached by Mrs. Comstock's first cousin, who was married to Beaufort's uncle, about finding Malvern a position at Whitehall. Beaufort had not yet found one but was actively looking. He had even taken the unusual step of interviewing Malvern to discover his strong suits. No one doubted such a staunch Tory as Beaufort would succeed.

Helena received a letter from her papa, explaining that he could not feel it possible to return to England. It was of particular importance at this time that he be on hand to keep an eye on his vineyards. They had not been taken over by the French, but such vile stunts as arson were possible. Naturally he did not want Moira to put herself in danger. Perhaps when she was feeling stouter . . .

Two days later, another letter from Spain arrived. He was entertaining a Mrs. Thorold, from Cornwall. She had been traveling in Spain when the war broke out and was having a wretched time finding a safe shelter. No mention was made of Mr. Thorold. Her companion was a Mrs. Duncan, relict of a bishop. It seemed the ladies were veteran travelers who could not stay home. They had been to Greece and Italy, to Portugal and France. "Like me, they are more comfortable where the sun occasionally shines," he wrote.

Mrs. Thorold featured largely in his following letters, while Moira was reduced to a postscript. Aylesbury had convinced Mrs. Thorold (and her companion) that they were safer at Viñedo Paraíso until the Frenchies were run out of the country once and for all. The next time Lady Helena called on Moira, she heard that Gagehot had gotten his promotion and his salary increase. "I'm not sure that was wise of your papa," she said coyly. "It might put ideas in my head."

"You must let Papa know if these ideas take root."

"I really ought to drop him a note, though he hasn't written to me in two weeks. Oh, did I tell you Lucy and I are thinking of taking a trip to the lake district? She's never been, and neither have I. Isn't that a coincidence? Of course, Mr. Everett will come along for escort. I know what you are thinking," she added, wagging a finger. "But Gagehot will not be coming. He's decided to buy a cottage. Now that he is to stay in England, he'll want more than a couple of rooms. He spends half his time out tramping through houses with an estate agent. After he's done your papa's sherry business, I mean."

This sounded remarkably like a man with plans of marriage. Helena left in good spirits. She always visited in the morning while Severn was at work. She kept Lady Hadley informed but never discussed the visits with her. As it now appeared likely Moira was about to pass out of her daily life, there seemed no point in bringing on an argument.

Severn usually returned from work early, and if Helena's projected outing sounded "interesting," he was as likely as not to take the afternoon off to accompany her. It did not escape her notice that what interested him was the duke's being of the party. Severn, who expressed a keen interest in art, had not found the opening of a new art exhibit of sufficient interest to attend. She had gone with his mama and the Comstocks. A sail down the Thames on Rutledge's yacht to visit Strawberry Hill, on the other hand, appeared to intrigue him despite his having visited Walpole's Gothic castle many times before.

"But you hate the water, Edward!" his mama pointed out.

"Nonsense. I should enjoy a sail in fine spring weather. Strawberry Hill is always worth another visit."

"Rutledge won't mind if you join us," Helena said. "He asked me to invite anyone I liked."

As arranged, they all went to Greenwich in the duke's post chaise. Severn could find nothing to object to in the duke's manner to Helena, or in hers to him. The trip to Greenwich passed without incident. There they met up with the rest of the party for lunch at a tavern. After, they all went for an obligatory look at the Royal Observatory. They climbed up Observatory Hill and looked down from its steep summit to the river below.

A short tour of the courtyard to see the mark showing zero meridian of longitude, which established accurate time throughout the world, was also necessary. Christopher Wren's Seamen's Hospital completed the tour, and they were off for their sail. Rutledge led the way to the pier, with Severn noticeably in the rear, dreading the water trip.

When they reached the yacht, he stared in consternation at a bewildering welter of masts, sails, and ropes, all precariously balanced on a long body that pitched to and fro even with the ship at anchor. The very boarding of the ship by an unsteady gangplank seemed perilous.

"What a beauty, Rutledge!" Helena exclaimed. "And we have a good, stiff breeze to move us along. It will be like my trip to England. Let us begin at once."

A quarter of an hour later they finally moved away from the dock. After this tedious delay, however, the sails billowed and the yacht skimmed along at an alarming speed. The Thames was as busy a thoroughfare as the paved roads. Other pleasure crafts were few, but the river was alive with ugly barges. A dozen times Severn found his hands gripping the rail, ready to jump overboard if the expected collision occurred.

Severn, like Rutledge, stuck by Helena's side, both of them vying to point out to her the various sights of the passing scene. "There is St. Dunstan's church. It was burned in the great fire, but Wren rebuilt it. Very fine," Severn said.

"That is St. Mary's," Rutledge corrected, and went on with a tale, possibly apocryphal, that Thomas à Becket was once priest of St. Mary's in olden times.

After what seemed a very long time, Severn recognized the stained-glass windows, the turrets, and the battlements of Strawberry Hill, and he felt a great wave of relief. With a last creaking of masts and settling of sails, the ship finally reached shore. The party climbed up the hill, looking ahead to the House. At closer range, it was seen to be a compact building, looking somewhat as if various blocks had been put together, the roofline crenellated, and spires attached at the corners.

"It is hardly a true example of Gothic architecture, of course," Severn said, shaking his head at such a bastardized thing. "It was Walpole's conceit to paste it together in the last century, using a little cottage as his starting point. He trimmed it up with bits and pieces from real Gothic buildings."

"Oh, but it is lovely!" Helena exclaimed. "I had not thought Englishmen had such imagination."

The other ladies found it enchanting and hastened toward the gates, eager to explore imagined dungeons and smoke-stained walls, with hopefully a ghost or two. It lacked these delights. Its interior was brightly finished in cream and gold, but it was supplied with sufficient stained glass, fan vaulting, and fireplaces resembling tombs that it found favor. For sixty minutes they all admired the house. There were stained-glass windows plundered from ancient buildings and set in lunettes above clear glass windows to give its builder a view of the surrounding countryside. Walpole had been a famous collector. Like a magpie, he surrounded his nest with what appealed to him: Cardinal Wolsey's red hat, jewels and coins, paintings and books and tapestries. Helena was much taken with the collection of spears, arrows, and broadswords, and particularly with the gold antelopes on the stairs.

"This is the staircase he used for inspiration in his novel *The Castle of Otranto*," Rutledge explained.

"What novel is that?" Helena asked. "I have not read it."

"I shall find you a copy," Rutledge promised.

"I have a signed copy in the study. You must have it, Cousin," Severn interjected.

"Speaking of writers," Rutledge said, taking her by the elbow, "you will want to run along and see Alexander Pope's grotto and garden."

"I expect the party would rather eat," Severn said, hoping to shorten the tour.

"I have had a picnic prepared," Rutledge announced. This was greeted with enthusiasm. "We shall eat down by the river, among the willows."

"I thought we would eat in the Barmy Arms," Severn objected. "No one wants to eat on the damp earth. The ladies will destroy their frocks."

"I have brought blankets," Rutledge replied.

"I hate picnics," Severn muttered.

Helena joined him. In a low voice she said, "You are behaving wretchedly, Severn. The duke has gone to a deal of trouble for his outing. I wish you would not spoil it."

"Only Rutledge would expect to feed his guests by a swampy river, amid the stench of fish and clouds of midges."

"It will be fine. You'll see," she said, and with this assurance she got him to the picnic grounds, where Rutledge's servant had arranged a lavish feast. After champagne, Severn began to think it was a tolerable idea.

"A pity we have not brought bathing costumes, and we could have a swim," Rutledge said.

"Let us do it sometime," Helena said. "I love swimming."

Severn said nothing, but his face said, You would!

"Do you swim, Eduardo?" she asked.

"I used to, when I was a child," he said, with a certain look at Rutledge.

Helena just smiled at his ill temper. "One never forgets. You should pitch yourself into the water one day. You won't drown. You'll see."

"What is the point?"

"What is the point of living, if you only mean to sit like a thundercloud when others are trying to enjoy themselves? You should pitch yourself into all of life, Eduardo, and enjoy it while you can. You'll be an old man soon enough."

It was entirely a novel experience for Severn to receive a lecture on working too hard. He soon imagined Helena was concerned on his behalf. After another glass of champagne, he began to think it was rather pretty here, with the ladies in their bonnets and bright gowns, the willows drooping beside them, while the water gleamed beyond. They lingered long by the river's edge, chatting idly. Some couples went for a stroll, but as Helena remained with Severn, Rutledge stayed behind, too.

The two gentlemen reminded her of a pair of dogs guarding a bone. She hoped Rutledge was not beginning to imagine she was in love with him, when she had told him very clearly she was not. It amused her to let Severn think she was, at any rate.

When all the walkers had returned, they boarded the yacht again and returned as the sun was sinking over the spires and rooftops of London. Severn had planned a trip to the theater for that evening, but after a day on the water, no one seemed much interested in it.

Helena, stifling a yawn, said, "I shall go home and write Papa a letter, then retire early."

When they reached Belgrave Square, Helena thanked Rutledge enthusiastically for the party.

"We shall have a bathing party one of these days," he promised. "Perhaps a weekend in Brighton—"

"Our weekends are all booked," Severn said firmly.

"It need not be a weekend," Helena said to the duke.

When Rutledge left and they entered the house, Severn suggested a quiet hand of cards to pass a few hours. Helena said, "I shall go up and write to Papa, as I mentioned."

"I shall work. I really shouldn't have taken the day off."

"Why did you, as it was patently obvious you did not enjoy the outing?"

"I think you know why," he said, offended, and went frowning into his office. Did that embrace in the carriage mean nothing to her? It could not be considered anything but a preamble to a proposal in England. Surely she was not changing her mind?

Chapter Eighteen

As Severn sat in his study, not catching up on missed work but gazing at his own reflection in the window, he pondered Helena's question and his own reply. What he should have said was that the reason he went was that he did not like her being with Rutledge. Did she have to ask such a question? He expected a more intuitive grasp of romance from a lady who performed that Spanish dance. Yet the simple fact was that she did not really seem to love him. His face, wavy from the imperfections in the old glass window, scowled back at him. Good God! Was that how he had looked all day? No wonder she had chided him.

The duke, he recalled, had smiled like a moonling, and Rutledge had never been an obliging fellow. Was there an understanding between them? Rutledge had not asked for permission to offer. He would never offer without permission. Severn sighed wearily. He had thought his courting days would be full of pleasure, but politics kept getting in his way. Yet he disliked to stop; Brougham had written to Hadley, and Hadley had expressed his delight in his son's work. Smoothing Papa's feelings was no longer necessary, now that he meant to marry Helena, yet he had been hoping to please his father on both fronts.

He really ought to arrange a special outing for Helena himself, something to outshine the trip to Strawberry Hill. His own preference was for a riding party, but Helena had mentioned she enjoyed bathing. Rutledge had suggested a trip to Brighton for the purpose. Why wait for Rutledge to provide that treat and weasel his way closer to Helena's heart? He would do it himself. His family did not own a house in Brighton. His papa had not been one of those who followed Prinny and his cronies to the seaside to raise hell, but he could hire a private parlor to provide a proper dinner. He would not ask Helena to eat off her lap at the smelly beach. They would leave in the morning in his curricle and enjoy an uninterrupted four hours of privacy. If the traffic was not too heavy, he would let Helena take the ribbons for a few miles. She would enjoy that.

They would return by moonlight the same evening, the two of them alone in the curricle for another private trip. It would be an auspicious occasion to make his formal proposal. He would take the family engagement ring with him. Once she had accepted his offer, Rutledge would stop pestering her.

He had to settle on a suitable day and select their guests. Marion, of course, and an escort for her. Her mama would be happy to join them as chaperon. He must invite Rutledge. He would be leaving for the Newmarket races next week. Severn had planned to attend himself, but he would be too busy. That was the time to have the bathing party, though, when Rutledge could not attend. After he had mentally selected a dozen other harmless souls, there remained only to choose the inn to provide dinner. The inn would make the bathing arrangements. Severn would not join the bathing. He would stay on the beach with blankets and a thermos of the coffee Helena liked so much, to assist the others when they came, shivering, from the water.

Severn went to his mama's room to discuss his plans with her the next morning before going downstairs. She was pleased to see him and urged him on with the best will in the world.

"Do it, before she decides she wants to be a duchess."

"I shall take the engagement ring to Hamlet this very day to have it cleaned. Or have one of the footmen do it for me, as it is a little out of my way."

This offhand speech denoted something less than the proper pitch of infatuation. "You *are* in love with her, Edward?"

"Of course, Mama. It is just that I have an important meeting this morning."

"Oh, dear, you sound just like your papa. I am happy to see you becoming serious, Edward, but don't become *too* serious."

His smile was as carefree as ever. "Small danger of that."

He went downstairs and broached his scheme to Helena over breakfast. "We must repay Rutledge for his hospitality. As he seemed interested in this trip to Brighton, and you, I think, agreed, it seemed proper for me to host the party."

His plan found approval at once. "What a splendid idea!" Helena smiled. "But will it be to your liking, Eduardo?"

"So long as it makes you happy," he said.

"I should like it, of all things. Are you sure you can be spared from Whitehall for a whole day?"

He basked in her approval and concern. "I daresay Parliament can do without me for one day."

"I must notify the ladies at once. They will want to have their bathing costumes made up."

"I have the list here," he said, handing it to her. With a memory of Rutledge's largess, he added, "If you wish to ask any of your own special friends, you must feel free to do so. Just let me know the number, so that I may inform the inn. I shall take care of inviting the gentlemen."

She glanced down the short list. "No, I cannot think of anyone else. You have included all my special friends, Eduardo. This is very thoughtful of you."

"I thought we might all drive down in our curricles, except for the chaperon, of course. Mrs. Comstock and Marion would prefer the closed carriage. Do you think you are up to handling the ribbons of my curricle, Cousin?"

"I don't see why not. I have handled the duke's bloods," she replied mischievously.

His smile was in some danger of freezing, but with a thought of the future, Severn maintained his equanimity. He left for work that morning with a smile. Helena immediately began writing up the invitations. As the day was fine, she decided to deliver them herself. The last one to be delivered was to the Comstocks. Mrs. Comstock invited her in for a cup of tea while she and Marion checked their calendar.

"Yes, it seems we are free of visits on that day," Marion said. "We were tentatively promised to take tea with Allan's aunt, but that can be put off." This speech was accompanied by a smile that gave the name Allan a certain significance. "You heard about Allan's great fortune?" she asked.

"I'm not sure what Allan you refer to," Helena replied.

"I mean Malvern, of course. Beaufort was highly impressed with him. Allan is to be the member for one of Beaufort's ridings in the next election. The election is a formality; he must campaign, but the outcome is assured. Meanwhile, Beaufort has taken him on as his private secretary to give him a notion how things are done in Parliament. He thinks Allan shows great promise, to judge by his salary. And after he is a member, there will be sinecures to give him a decent income."

"I always thought Malvern showed great promise," Mrs. Comstock said. "He is a man of amazing ingenuity. Do you remember how he found that teapot to match my set when it got broken, Marion? So very obliging. I'm sure he must have visited a dozen shops, for the pattern was discontinued decades ago. He wouldn't take a penny for it either."

"And the wheel for your carriage, Mama," Marion added.

"That, too. The wheeler wanted to sell me a new one at an outrageous price. Malvern got one the proper size from the carriage of a friend whose rig had overturned and was hors de combat. He even had it painted to match my carriage."

"I take it you have been seeing a good deal of Malvern," Helena said. Their smirks and smiles told her the romance was on the boil and approaching a conclusion, if it had not done so already. "Are congratulations in order, Marion?"

"Not yet," Mrs. Comstock replied, "but he has let

me know his intentions are honorable. He would like to be a part of this outing Severn has arranged. Beaufort will be happy to give him a day off, for he works him like a slave."

"Then may I tell Severn you three will be coming? He hoped you would join us as well, Mrs. Comstock, to play propriety."

"I shall be happy to go. We shall take Malvern in our rig," she said. "It is nice to have a dependable gentleman in the carriage for such outings."

Helena left in a little consternation. Malvern, she knew, was anathema to Severn, but how could she deny Marion's chosen escort? Severn would not be happy with the match, but when Mrs. Comstock was so deep in the throes of passion, it seemed unlikely Severn would have anything to say about it. In any case, Malvern seemed to be setting himself a new course. If he did not actually love Marion, he at least liked her. Marion, she felt, had enough love for them both. She was hardly the same daunting girl she had been a few weeks ago.

As it was still early, Lady Helena decided to visit Moira to see how her romance was progressing. She would be leaving soon for the lake district, so this might be a farewell visit. Moira was alone but dressed to go out, with her pelisse and a new high poke bonnet sitting beside her on the sofa.

"Ah, Helena. Just the lady I hoped to see," she said, smiling from ear to ear. Her old languor and tired eyes were replaced by smiling and clear-eyed vivacity.

"I shan't keep you a moment, for I see you are going out."

"Yes, Lucy and I are going shopping."

"For your trip, I daresay?"

"That has been put off, I fear. Perhaps next year."

As Moira had spoken of the visit with great enthusiasm, Helena wondered that she was in such good spirits at its cancellation. "I am sorry to hear it. I trust there is nothing amiss with the Everetts?"

"Quite the contrary. The Everetts are going. Lester and I have decided to go in a different direction, to Cornwall. He says that although he has been to the continent a dozen times, he has never seen half his own country, so we are going west. What do you think of that, eh?"

Helena thought it pretty fast behavior for the couple to be traveling alone together. "Why don't the Everetts accompany you to Cornwall?" she asked.

"Naughty girl! I see what you are thinking, but it is no such a thing. We are to be married first." She wiggled her left hand, on which a small diamond sparkled.

Helena did not have to simulate her pleasure. "I am delighted for you!" she exclaimed, and rose to hug her friend.

"We both know someone who will not be so happy," Moira said, with a little sigh. "I have written Algernon. I do hope he won't take the news too hard. Anything you can do to help would be appreciated, dear. It would be a tragedy if he let Lester go. We count on his salary. Not that he could not be hired by another company, for he is an excellent salesman!"

"Papa would not be so petty, Moira. He speaks most highly of Mr. Gagehot. When are you planning the wedding?"

"Next Wednesday. I do hope you will come. It is to take place at two in the afternoon."

"Where will you be married?"

"At St. Peter's, a little chapel near Lucy's place, just a small wedding, but with a proper feast after. Lester and I have been so busy fixing up the house that we haven't time for a fancy wedding. Well, it's the second time for us both, and it's not quite the same as the first, is it?"

"You've found a house. Do tell me about it."

"Lester found a little house for us on Maddox Street, just east of New Bond, so handy for shopping. The house is small, mind, but it's not as though we'll be setting up a nursery at our age. Solid brick, with a tidy parlor and every stitch in it brand new. Isn't it exciting!"

"It sounds lovely, Moira. I am so happy for you."

"About a wedding gift, dear, if your papa should ask what we'd like, tell him he mustn't worry about that. Money will do just fine. I wouldn't mention it, except that Lester was afraid he might go sending us some rare vintage sherry, as he did for his foreman in Spain. Our friends wouldn't appreciate it, and we really don't drink that much. Lester prefers ale for every day, and you know I hardly take a sip at all now."

"You are to be congratulated. I shall tell Papa not to tempt you in that respect."

"A pity he couldn't know sooner, for I could use the cash. My trousseau, you know. A lady likes to have something a little special for the treacle moon."

Helena took the hint and wrote out a check for a hundred pounds on her papa's behalf. It was what she thought proper for an old employee like Gagehot. She wrote down the address of the chapel and the time of the wedding, then left.

As she drove home, it was borne in on her that several ladies of her acquaintance were tying up their future, while she still remained unsettled. She was eager to get on with finding a mate and settling down, but somehow no one she had met thus far quite pleased her. Rutledge was nice. A duke, but not what she thought of as a great man, or ever likely to be one. Perhaps Severn would do after all. He seemed to be coming down off his high horse. It was rather sweet of him to arrange this Brighton party to please her.

She returned to tell Lady Hadley of Moira's romance.

"It is done!" she exclaimed. "The nuptials are announced!"

"My dear *Cousina.* You mean Edward has come up to scratch! I never thought he had the gumption. Indeed I was by no means sure you would have him, for you always speak of love as well as of finding a great man. Personally I have never found the two go together. I mean to say, who could love Lord Liverpool, or any of the royal dukes, or any of the great men we have in England, come to that?"

Helena stared in confusion. "Edward? And me? Oh, no, ma'am. You misunderstand me. I am speaking of Mrs. Petrel-Jones and Gagehot. Where did you get the idea—"

"Oh, my dear, he has been scheming himself blue in the face to outdo Rutledge. Why do you think he set on next week for the trip to Brighton?

"I assumed it was the only day he could get away."

"The first day he was sure Rutledge would be

away. The Newmarket races. Edward senses stiff competition from him."

"Does he indeed?" Helena said through thin lips.

"Why, he even sent the engagement ring in for cleaning, to beat Rutledge to the punch. The pièce de résistance, you see. He would have taken it himself, but he had a meeting."

Helena was furious with Severn. All his fine talk of repaying Rutledge's hospitality. Severn wasn't doing this to please her, but to put her in a good mood to accept his offer because he felt she and her fortune would be a benefit to his political career. And he did not even take the ring to be cleaned himself!

"And did he say he was madly in love with me, ma'am?"

"He did not say *madly*. But when I asked him, he said yes. I am delighted, my dear. You are not a bit Spanish, and so well dowered. Severn always looks to the balance sheet these days. It is his job to do so. Hadley will be in alt."

Lady Hadley's comments put the news of Malvern's success out of Helena's mind. She went abovestairs to indulge in some schemes of her own. So Eduardo was scheming to attach her dowry, was he? Her first thought was to push the day of the Brighton trip forward so that Rutledge could attend. As the invitations had been issued already, however, this was impossible. The other possibility was to persuade Rutledge to postpone his departure for one day. She would ask him very nicely that evening at Mrs. Forrest's ball.

Chapter Nineteen

"I have a filly running, so I really must be at Newmarket by next week," Rutledge explained when Helena hinted that he might delay his departure. "A sweet three-year-old. She needs the experience before the derby later in the month."

A four-legged filly obviously took precedence over a two-legged one. Helena's mind was easy on one score, at least. The duke was not in love with her. Her next effort to annoy Severn was to ask Malvern to stand up with her for the waltzes. Severn did not know how matters stood between Malvern and Marion.

"Why am I honored by this sudden attention?" Malvern asked bluntly.

"I am angry with Severn and want to teach him a lesson."

"That usually spells trouble for me. What are you up to, vixen?"

She hardly knew, but she knew she wanted to make Severn angry and jealous, and if Rutledge would not oblige her, she would use Malvern. "Just repaying Severn's own trick of pretending partiality where none exists."

"My better instincts urge me to inquire why you suppose he is merely pretending?"

She tossed her curls. "Give me credit for knowing the difference, sir."

"Don't go pretending to Marion we are involved in some clandestine affair. Charming as you are . . ." He let his words dwindle out.

"After your hard work finding teapots and fixing wheels, you would not want to risk losing her," she teased.

"I would not want to lose her in any case. I happen to love the lady." Then he smiled and added, "Or nearly love her. She grows more agreeable by the day. And I do love being treated with the consideration I find at Grosvenor Square. The Comstocks are making a man of me, Lady Helena. Don't do anything to jeopardize it, I pray."

"On the contrary, I will do whatever is in my power to help. I, too, find Marion improves on acquaintance. And so do you, Allan," she added with a smile in which flirtation was transformed to genuine fondness. "May I call you Allan?"

"Only if you allow me to call you Helena."

"Please do, until you can call me Cousin."

Severn saw this bantering interchange and came pouncing forward to draw her away as soon as the set was over.

"I have asked you not to encourage that scoundrel, Cousin," he said severely.

"The rest of society does not judge him so harshly, Severn."

He scowled. Helena called him Severn only when she was annoyed with him. He particularly liked to hear her call him Eduardo, in her soft Spanish way.

"In fact," she continued, "Malvern is in the process of being reformed. He has found a position with Beaufort and will stand for office at the next election. Why, I shouldn't be surprised if he turns out to be one of our great men, in time."

"Malvern is a dubious proposition at best."

"Making a worldly match is no longer so important with me. I do feel, however, that with the right lady behind him, he will do very well in the world."

"Damn, the man's a Tory!" he exclaimed.

"Yes, he is with the right party to advance his career."

"I think you encourage the fellow only to vex me!"

"That is the trouble with you, Severn. You always think when you should feel." Why did he not forbid her to see Malvern? He might at least have threatened a duel, so that she could throw herself on his chest and forbid it. She strode angrily away, leaving Severn behind to ponder this development.

A judicious question dropped here and there told him that Malvern was indeed working for Beaufort and was to stand for member soon. It was inconceivable to him that Malvern had changed his stripes for any other reason but to win Helena. He doubted the reformation would continue once he had his hands on her money. And she, like a fool, was taken in by him.

He danced with all the prettiest debs before suggesting to Helena that it was time to go home. He fully expected an argument, but she agreed at once. She met Marion in the coatroom when she went for her cape.

"Allan told me you are unhappy with Severn," she said. "I don't want you using Malvern to teach him a lesson."

"I can teach him a lesson all by myself. He is too insufferable, Marion, pretending to care for me

174

when his real motive is to outdo Rutledge." She explained about the outing to Brighton.

Marion, having suffered a few snubs from Severn in the past, was not averse to encouraging Helena. "It is your fortune Severn is after, of course," she said, so matter-of-factly it almost sounded as if she had been told so, "but it is obvious he likes you. What is wrong in that?"

"What is wrong is that he is not telling the truth. He is acting a lie in this Brighton affair. He actually had the engagement ring cleaned to present to me," she said, full of indignation.

Marion frowned. "That is rather sweet. You must remember the English are different from what you are used to, Cousin. They do not rant and rave and strut their passion, but I assure you they feel quite as deeply as the Latin races."

This may have been true for Malvern, but Helena doubted Severn had a passionate atom in his body. "Let us see if we can raise some vestige of it," she said.

"It sounds as if you are trying to make him jealous. Why bother, if you don't care for him?"

"I don't care for him in the least," Helena said angrily. "*Santo Dios,* do you think I could ever love that iceberg! There is no natural feeling in him. He schemes and plans everything, even his love life. Love should overwhelm a man. He should not coolly *plan* it all and get a ring cleaned. He should not be able to stop himself from flowing over with—" She came to a stop as she realized Marion was staring in astonishment.

"Yes, I can see you have no feelings for him," Marion said, with an ironic look.

"*Caramba,* I am mad with annoyance. That is all." She snatched up her cloak and left.

There was little conversation as the carriage wended its way to Belgrave Square. "I have a wretched headache," Helena announced as soon as they were inside the house.

"These headaches are becoming more frequent," Severn said suspiciously. "You ought to see a doctor, Cousin."

She glared. "I shall require some more funds tomorrow, Severn," she said coolly. "I have written a check for that hundred pounds you put in my account last week."

"Already? What did you buy?" he demanded.

She looked down her little nose and said, "I do not have to account to you for my purchases. Pray arrange for some more money. I require it immediately."

"You've run through your allowance. I would have to sell some consols."

"Then do it."

"You have been spending a great deal of money," he said. "Of course, you have had your gowns and a carriage. . . . It seems a shame to dip into your capital."

"Money is for spending, is it not?"

"That is its ultimate use, certainly, but . . . You could sell your tilbury and use Mama's carriage," he suggested.

She sneered. "Too kind, but I do not wish to be at the mercy of someone else when I want an outing."

"Just where do you go on these outings?" he asked. Worry lent a touch of asperity to his tone. "I know Marion has not been accompanying you much recently."

"I call on friends," she replied vaguely.

"Have you loaned Malvern money?" he asked.

"Certainly not."

"It would not surprise me if he tried to borrow from you."

"You misunderstand the matter, sir. It is only *you* who takes such a keen interest in my fortune."

"One of us has to, when it is obvious you have no notion of management." He heard the echo of his father in that speech and regretted it. He knew how demeaning such scolds were.

"That need not concern you, milord." On this challenging speech she turned and whisked upstairs.

In her unhappiness and confusion, she was beginning to toy with the idea of returning to Spain. England was the wrong climate for her. The people were too heartless and mercenary. Rutledge, who claimed to love her, would not do this one little thing that she asked. Malvern was marrying Marion for her dot and only trying to convince himself it was love. As to Severn, the man was a walking balance sheet. How dare he suggest she sell her carriage!

His real aim was to keep her interned all day while he went to Whitehall. This one outing he had planned for her pleasure was a sham. It was nothing else but a business trip, whose goal was to soften her up to accept his hateful offer. Just so did Papa ply the sherry buyers with his best sherry, and when they were light-headed with wine, they signed larger orders than they had intended. Of course they got their money's worth. It was excellent sherry! "Just oiling the wheels" was how her papa explained it.

And Severn was just oiling the wheels for this merger he desired with her fortune. She enjoyed a brief imagining of how he would go about it. They would be driving home from Brighton in the open carriage, tired and sated after a full day. Moonlight would bathe them in a ghostly glow. He would take her hand and say, "Did you enjoy your party, Cousin?"

She would smile and simper, "It was charming, Eduardo."

"My only thought is to make you happy," he would say, drawing to a stop in some romantic spot overlooking the water. (Her sense of geography was vague.) Then he would take her in his arms and kiss her as he had kissed her that evening she had danced the *jota*. A sad smile seized her lips as she remembered that evening. It might very well have worked. It was well she knew why he "loved" her, or she might have found herself shackled for life to an accountant who would not even allow her to keep her own carriage.

But she would not let him have his way. She would not go to Brighton, that's all. Why should she play into his hands? She would be ill on that day at the last minute, so that Severn could not call it off. It must be no serious ailment, as she meant to be well again for Moira's wedding party on Wednesday and, of course, her own ball on Friday.

Belowstairs Severn sat alone in his study, prey to his own imaginings. Things were not going as he had hoped at all. He had assumed Helena had heeded his warning and kept away from Malvern. It now seemed possible, indeed likely, that she had been sneaking around corners to meet him. The heartlessness of her, using Marion as a dupe. Of course, she had never liked Marion above half. This talk of reformation and Malvern's being a great man was troubling. That is what came of allowing ladies too much freedom. He must get rid of her carriage. Selling it without her agreement would bring things to an unpleasant head. No saying what the hothead would do.

He must be more clever than that. He would incapacitate the carriage in some manner. It would be only for a short while. He still hoped, in spite of all, that they would return from Brighton as a formally engaged couple, at which time she would naturally do as he asked. Like Helena, he allowed himself a daydream of that return trip from Brighton. Unlike her, he knew they would not be driving by the sea on their trip north. He had chosen the exact spot where he would make his proposal.

There was an inn just outside of Gatwick, halfway home, where the party would stop for refreshment. He would spring his team and reach it a quarter of an hour before the others joined them. It was during that interval that he meant to whisk out the diamond ring and get it on her finger. During the ensuing daydream, he gave not a thought to confiscating either her fortune or her carriage. Indeed he even regretted that she was so well to grass. He would like to heap unaccustomed pleasures and treasures on her head, to see her smile and say, "Oh, Eduardo!"

He opened his desk drawer to look at the ring. Beside it, nestled in silver paper, sat the lock of her hair he had retrieved from the side table in the saloon. He stroked it, as though it were a talisman, promising luck in his endeavor. He meant to have it mounted somehow in a piece of sentimental jewelry as a keepsake. When those sable curls had silvered, this would remind him of their youth.

Chapter Twenty

After ordering the groom to take Lady Helena's carriage in for repairs, Severn left for work early on Monday. The first she learned of it was when she called for her tilbury at ten o'clock and was told it was being repaired.

"It was in perfect repair," she said in confusion.

"His lordship mentioned the wheels needed tightening, and you could use her ladyship's carriage if you had to go out."

His lordship! Helena went with nostrils pinched in vexation to ask her godmother if she might take her carriage.

"Certainly, my dear, I never go out before noon. But what is amiss with your own rig? Not had an accident, I hope?"

"Severn decided it needed repairs," she replied.

"Up to his tricks, is he? His papa used to try such stunts on me to curb my activities. You may be sure Edward suspects you of secret assignations with a gentleman. Really, it is most annoying of him. That is no way to win a lady."

"I wish you will tell him so. He pays no heed to me."

"And as he has not offered yet, you would not like to let him know you are onto him, I daresay.

It is best to lay down your rules before accepting him; then you can always fling them in his face if he tries to shorten the reins later. I wish someone had given me advice before I married Hadley."

"It is not too late to lay down some rules now."

"Ah, well, we have reached a modus vivendi, and it hardly seems worthwhile upsetting things, but I shall enjoy watching you bring Edward to heel, *Cousina*. You have my blessing—and my carriage. Where are you going?"

"To buy a wedding gift for Moira and Gagehot. The check I gave was really from Papa. He will repay me the money, so there was no need for Severn to rip up at me for spending too much."

"You did not tell him the reason?"

"Certainly not. It is my own business."

"Much the best way. The less they know, the better. If you are short of funds, I shall be happy to oblige you."

"I have enough to buy a little something for Moira, but if Severn fails to fill up my account, I may have to apply to you for a loan, *Madrina*. He was unhappy to sell my consols."

"I don't know why gentlemen are always so reluctant to sell consols. Hadley is the same. What good are they? They never increase in value like a stock on the exchange. They just sit there forever, giving you a bare five percent."

"There is no accounting for it. I shall be home for lunch," Helena said, and took her leave.

It was Lady Hadley's groom who drove the carriage and her footmen who accompanied Helena to the shops. After a deal of looking, she settled on a silver epergne. As she would not be seeing Moira again before the wedding, she asked the clerk to wrap it, and she delivered it herself that same morning.

"How lovely!" Moira exclaimed. "You shouldn't have, dear."

They talked for ten minutes. Moira showed her guest the gown she had had made up for the wedding. It was an ornate silk affair in pale peach, with more than sufficient lace and ribbons. Helena praised it, declined tea, then rose to leave.

"You'll be at the wedding, I hope?" Moira asked.

"Certainly."

"Bring Severn, if you think he would like to come."

"Thank you, but I shall come alone. Severn is so busy."

From Moira's, Helena went straight home. In the afternoon, a few gentlemen dropped in. She was sorry they had left by the time Severn returned, for she wanted to display her popularity. He went directly to his study and called for the footman who had accompanied Helena that morning, to discover her itinerary.

That she had been out shopping when her pockets were to let was annoying but only what he expected of a lady. It was the second stop that piqued his curiosity. "Upper Grosvenor Square? Who the devil could she be visiting there?"

"And delivering a present. I had a look at the cards posted in the lobby." He had also copied down the names and drew out a slip of paper to read them. When he came to Mrs. Petrel-Jones, Severn held up his hand. "No need to go further. Thank you, Scallion, you have done well." He flipped a coin to the delighted footman and went in search of Helena.

He found her alone in the library, scanning the journals. In his agitation, he failed to notice it was the schedule of ships leaving London that she was studying. She hastily closed the journal and turned a stiff face to greet him.

"Severn, I should like to know why you sent my carriage off for repairs without telling me when it is virtually new."

"I asked Sugden to explain. I noticed a loose wheel."

"When did you notice it? You have not seen it for days."

"Actually, I had my groom look it over. I made sure Mama's carriage was available for you, as it seems you cannot pass a single day indoors."

"Why should I sit twiddling my thumbs all day?"

"There are more useful activities—reading, music. . . ."

She gave an angry snort. "Who can be bothered with that when it is so fine outdoors?"

"Why indeed, when you could be out spending money you don't have," he retorted hotly. "And worse, visiting Mrs. Petrel-Jones, taking her gifts."

"I see you have set your minions to spy on me."

"I asked you not to associate with that woman."

"I took note of your request, milord," she replied with awful courtesy. "I did not choose to oblige you in the matter."

Her very calmness only served to raise his temper. "By God, you'll do as I say while you are under my roof."

"I am under your father's roof, sir, not under your thumb. If you think to dominate me by such absurd stunts as taking away my carriage, you are very much mistaken."

"We'll see how you manage when I take away your money. Those dirty dishes you choose to associate with will find you less attractive when you cannot shower them with gifts. They are only out to fleece you, Helena."

"You must not judge my friends by your low standards, sir. Not everyone considers money the be-all and end-all."

"We'll see about that. I have not sold your consols, and I have no intention of doing so."

She smiled snidely. "Do you mean to drive me into the hands of the loan sharks, milord? I doubt I would have much trouble raising the wind."

"I forbid you to go to the cent percenters! Good God, you go from one freakish stunt to another. Have you no sense?"

Her eyes flashed dangerously. "I have sense enough to realize you are a tyrant, sir," she shot back. "But you will not tyrannize *me*. And furthermore, I have no intention of going on that stupid picnic to Brighton. You timed it on purpose to exclude Rutledge, after pretending you were arranging it to repay him for Strawberry Hill."

"I planned it for you, not Rutledge."

"No, sir, you planned it for yourself, thinking I would be foolish enough to accept an offer from you if you got me into the proper frame of mind. You don't con me so easily. If you think I am to be had for a picnic, you are very much mistaken."

Guilt rose to anger, and his reply was sharp. "That is rather previous of you, Cousin, declining an offer that has not been made. What makes you think I would offer for you? You have no sense, no propriety, no gratitude, an extremely disagreeable temperament, and—"

"And an extremely agreeable fortune. I did not mean to imply you cared for me. I know you better than to accuse you of human feelings. The whole world knows what interests *you*."

Crushed by her blanket condemnation, Severn found no option but to stiffen up and repeat his first statements. Her carriage was, unfortunately, hors de combat, and also her fortune. This said, he turned on his heel and strode from the room.

Helena angrily reopened the journal at the marine listings. It was patently impossible for her to continue living in this house. She never wanted to see Severn again. England was a bore. She had had a much nicer time in Spain. She took up a pen, dipped it in ink, and underlined one sailing. The *Princess Margaret* set sail for Spain the day after her ball. She would pay a secret visit to the Admiralty and arrange passage. They often took a few civilians, businessmen and such things. How could she endure the waiting?

She felt tears gathering in her eyes and cast the journal aside to flee to her room. She never cried. She would not let anyone see her in this moment of weakness.

Severn went to his study and poured a glass of claret to steady his shaking hands. His whole mind was in turmoil. What did one do with a female who had obviously been reared with no more care than a cat? The girl was completely out of control. After a second glass of wine, he decided that sterner measures were called for. What was the point of taking away her carriage and allowing her the freedom of his mama's? He learned where she had gone after the fact, but that was of no use. Tomorrow Mama's carriage would be taken to the shop for repairs as well. He would set Sugden to spying on her. If she left the house on foot, he would have her followed. If she ventured within a block of the moneylenders, he would have her pulled away by main force. He was not about to be beaten by a chit of a girl.

He pondered a long while over the projected party to Brighton. He would not, indeed could not, force her to go. As his only reason for undertaking this unpleasant excursion was to indulge her, he had no compunction in canceling it. Important business at Whitehall served as an excuse. How did she know he planned to propose? What had he said to tip her the clue? And how had she learned he timed the trip to avoid Rutledge's attendance? She was too sharp by half. A pity she did not put her wits to better use.

It was unusual for Severn to go out of his way to help anyone. He expected gratitude, not animosity. She was blind to his every effort to help her but could see no fault in these infra dig friends, the likes of Petrel-Jones and Malvern, who were only using her. He remembered the money falling from the chair at El Cafeto and wondered about it. He remembered she had been fumbling in her reticule. She had been leaving that money for Malvern.

After all his superficial mental ranting, he settled down to the real problem. Helena obviously despised him, and in spite of all, he still wanted to marry her. She would be a wickedly troublesome wife, and just at that period of his life when he was ready to assume the onus of his position. She misjudged him at every turn, imputing faults where virtue lurked. He did not want her money; he just disliked to see her duped. Oh, Lord, how often had he cringed to hear his papa say the same thing?

But it was unkind and unjust to accuse him of fortune hunting—and a demmed hard accusation to disprove.

Was it so bad of him to try to cut out Rutledge? All's fair in love and war, folks said. He walked slowly to the library, mentally rehearsing what he would say. The room was empty. He went in anyway, to be where she had recently been. An echo of her perfume hung in the air. He glanced at the journal, curious to see what had interested her. The marine listings. She had underlined a ship going to Spain, the *Princess Margaret*. She must be arranging to send those jackets she had had made up for her papa. She spoke highly of Aylesbury. How had she not come to cuffs with him?

No doubt she had him firmly under control, but she would find an English husband less pliable. He was still adamant that she must be tamed before he married her, but he began to wonder if it might not be accomplished by kindness rather than severity. He had never paid any heed to Papa's lectures. He would not mention the recent argument. He would be kind but firm.

Chapter Twenty-one

Lady Hadley had guests in for dinner that evening. Severn, seated at the head of the table with Helena at his left side, tried in vain to win favor with kindness. She bestowed only the briefest of replies to any comment or query before turning her conversation to her other partner. At the theater after dinner he continued being solicitous, offering to bring her wine at the intermission.

"Thank you, Severn, but I prefer to stretch my legs." A smile of pleasure lit his face until she added, "Lord Dufferin has offered to accompany me." Severn managed a smile as she left, but it was an impatient smile. He was Severn again.

When they arrived home, Lady Hadley announced she was for the feather tick. "Shall we have a glass of wine before retiring, Cousin?" Severn suggested, ever hopeful.

"You go ahead. I shall go upstairs with *Madrina*." She would have added an insult had his mama not been with them.

A strange lethargy came over Helena the next day. Despite the sunlight streaming in at the window, she did not ask about the availability of a carriage. Her unhappy thoughts were already halfway to Spain. Her heart felt heavy and sore within her.

She had received a letter from Papa, in which he announced his engagement to Mrs. Thorold, to take place in July. It made an excellent excuse for returning. She knew it was a good thing for Papa and tried to be happy for him. For herself, she knew things would not be the same with a young wife ruling the house. Mrs. Thorold, Papa wrote, was "plenty young enough to give me that heir our relatives are always nagging me about."

In her room, she idly thumbed through her gowns, deciding what to take with her. She would take some of her mama's pretty Spanish gowns and leave behind the hated white deb's gowns. She was interrupted by Sally, now noticeably blond but still wearing her freckles.

"Miss Comstock is downstairs, milady. She wants to know if you'd like to go out for a drive."

"I might as well," Helena said idly.

When she went to the carriage, she saw Malvern was there. She did not see Sugden send for a footman to follow them.

"Not working, Allan?" she asked, surprised.

"I am to take notes at a meeting for Beaufort tonight, so he has given me the afternoon off. We plan a drive out the Chelsea Road and a stop for tea. Mrs. Comstock could not come."

She was sunk to being a chaperon! "Would it be too much trouble to stop at the Admiralty? I want to arrange transport back to Spain. I have decided to return," she announced.

Her announcement was received with clamorous objections. "Why would you want to leave England? Spain is at war!"

"The war does not bother us much at the *viñedo*. I cannot remain at Belgrave Square. And you must

189

not breathe a *word* to Severn. Promise me on your heart you will not tell him."

They promised, though they both felt the threat was a mere love of dramatics on Helena's part. She would not really leave.

Malvern accompanied her to the Admiralty offices, then returned to wait with Marion in the carriage. An Admiral Henshaw, after the requisite warning of danger, agreed to book Lady Helena passage on the *Princess Margaret*. She returned to the carriage and they drove through the countryside to a Tudor inn tucked in under a cooling spread of elms.

"I was sorry Severn had to postpone his outing to Brighton," Marion said.

It was the first Helena had heard of it. She didn't know whether to be incensed or flattered. Had Severn postponed it because she had refused to go?

"That is the way with us working gentlemen," Malvern said. "I doubt I could have gotten away myself."

Marion poured tea. As her left hand flew often to hold the lid or straighten a cup, it was not long before Helena espied a chip of diamond on her finger.

"Is that an engagement ring!" she exclaimed.

Marion smiled softly. "We plan to marry very soon."

"May I be one of the first to congratulate you. I hope you will be very happy, Marion. And dear Allan."

Marion gushed on with details. "Allan wants to wait until he has a better-paying position, but Mama thinks the sooner the better. If we are married before Allan stands for Parliament, I can help him campaign."

Helena watched Malvern as she spoke, wondering if he would reveal any signs of regret. She could see only pleasure beaming from his eyes. It looked like genuine pleasure, even love.

After a leisurely tea, they drove back to Belgrave Square. Helena was in her room when Severn returned later. "About her ladyship . . ." Sugden said importantly, taking Severn's hat and gloves. Severn lifted a black brow. A terrible feeling of doom came over him at the butler's ominous tone.

Sugden revealed that her ladyship had gone out with Miss Comstock and a young gentleman whose description sounded dangerously like that of Malvern. They had gone to the Admiralty, then out the Chelsea Road to the Thorn and Thistle for tea.

Alone at an inn with that scoundrel? "Miss Comstock accompanied them to this inn?" he asked, blood rising up to his ears, where it caused a hammering sensation.

"Yes, milord. Her ladyship was never alone with the man."

"That will be all, Sugden. Thank you. Have Lady Helena followed until further notice. And see that the footman is given funds to cover the expense of hiring a hansom cab."

Severn went to his study, where he sat with his head in his hands and a knot in his stomach, thinking. Would a trip to the Admiralty be necessary only to send her father his jackets, or did Malvern's presence indicate they were booking passage for Spain together? He disliked to sully Helena's reputation by making inquiries at the Admiralty. Word might get out.

Severn was not one for laissez-faire politics. When a troublesome situation confronted him, he preferred to meet it head-on. He would ask Helena about this trip to the Admiralty with Malvern. Common sense told him it would be a stormy interview, very likely ending with Helena running to her room. He would let her have her dinner first and confront her after.

His kindness diminished to mere civility over dinner. A query as to her day brought an admission that she had driven out with Marion. Not a word of Malvern, the deceitful creature! He expected to see signs of mischief in her demeanor and wondered at her listlessness. Lady Hadley told him of Algernon's pending marriage. She did not mention Helena's intention of attending it, for the very good reason that Helena had not told her.

She said, "Did I tell you, *Cousina*? Your papa's jackets have arrived from Weston. How will you get them to him?"

"That is arranged," Helena replied. She meant to take them with her.

As they dined alone, Severn dispensed with his port and asked Helena into his office immediately after dinner. She agreed without pleasure and without any apparent misgivings.

She didn't take a seat but just asked, "What is it, Severn?" as soon as they were in the room.

"You were out with Malvern today," he said accusingly.

He watched as her spine stiffened and a flash of anger shot from her dark eyes. "What of it? I am not a prisoner, I hope? Marion asked me to accompany them on a drive. As I have no carriage of my own, I must take what transportation I can."

"May I inquire why you went to the Admiralty?"

"You have been spying on me! This is intolerable."

His hands flashed out and grasped her wrists in a painful grip as she turned away. "Are you planning to slip away to Spain with him? Is that it? Sneaking behind my back!"

She wrenched her wrists free. "How dare you lay a hand on me, sir! For your information, Malvern is betrothed to Marion—not that it is any concern of yours whom I marry!"

"What! Marion and Malvern?" He sensed a trick here.

"Anyone with an eye in his head can see they are in love. Good God, why do you think he has suddenly become a pattern card of industry, finding a position and standing for Parliament? They plan to marry very soon."

The news was so unexpected, yet so welcome, that Severn hardly knew what to say. It was welcome, of course, for removing Malvern as a rival. "When did this come about? Surely Mrs. Comstock has not given her consent?"

"It is Mrs. Comstock who wants an early wedding. She is half in love with him herself. You have a very wrong impression of Malvern if you think this is a case of cream-pot love, Severn. He is sincerely attached to Marion."

"Attached to her dowry is more like it."

Her nostrils pinched in distaste. "All things look yellow to the jaundiced eye," she retorted.

Severn considered his position and realized he looked not only a fool, but a tyrant. In fact, his depriving Helena of her carriage might very well pitch her into seeking company that he disliked.

And now that Malvern was out of the way, he had nothing to fear. Rutledge, he knew, had left for Newmarket. The fear and anger that had made his dinner such a trial dissipated, to be replaced by a feeling very like euphoria.

"I'm sorry, Helena, about your carriage."

"You were overly interfering, Severn."

"I daresay you are right. I have not had a young lady under my protection before. Your being from a foreign country made me fear you were not aware of all our conventions."

He went to his desk and poured two glasses of wine without asking whether she wanted one. When he handed one to her, she hesitated a moment, then accepted it and sat down. Her mind was rushing ahead to other possible questions. If he asked why she had gone to the Admiralty, what could she say to fool him?

Strangely, Severn did not even mention it. He assumed it had to do with dispatching her papa's jackets. Having blundered into one egregious error, he had no intention of further humiliating himself. His mind now was on mending fences.

"Your ball is this Friday," he said, trying for a cheerful topic. "I trust we won't have to postpone it, as we postponed the Brighton trip?" He ventured a smile.

"That won't be necessary. I should like to invite Malvern, if a dispensation for this special occasion is possible?" she asked, with gentle irony.

"We can hardly leave out Marion's fiancé. I feel she is making an error, but—"

Helena set her glass on the desk with a thump. "Is it not usual for a critic to have some knowledge of that which he criticizes? What do you know about

194

love, Severn? Stick to politics and finance. Your expertise in love is sorely lacking." She rose and strode briskly from the room without a backward glance.

She had no desire to go out that evening, but they were promised to a musical soiree at Lady Melbourne's, and to claim a megrim might very well bring a doctor down on her head. It would be a quiet evening, at least. A young lady was allowed to look blue at such dull dos, when she could be out dancing. And she would be spared making meaningless conversation.

She used the concert to plan her escape. She would remain in London for Moira's wedding tomorrow and her own ball on Friday. Saturday the *Princess Margaret* set sail for Spain, and she would be on it. She could not leave without thanking *Madrina*. She must leave her a note.

Severn, watching her from the corner of his eye while the Italian soprano sang, wondered what had brought that sad expression to Helena's face. Was she, like him, unhappy with this breach in their romance? What could he do to win her back?

When they reached home, she immediately headed for the staircase. "A moment, Cousin," he said.

She turned and looked at him coolly. "Your carriage has been repaired," he said. "You may feel free to go out tomorrow—without being followed." A blush rose up his throat to acknowledge his past folly.

"Thank you. And my funds? Have they, too, been restored?"

"I shall arrange it tomorrow. How much will you require?"

"One hundred pounds should do it."

"If you are in a hurry, I should like to loan you the money. It takes a few days to sell consols, you must know."

"Again, thank you. Naturally I shall repay you before . . . before long," she said. The words "before I leave" had nearly slipped out. "A few days" might turn out to be a week, and she wanted to pay for her passage as soon as possible. She had been giving her flight much thought, and it occurred to her that the sooner she began sneaking her trunks down to the ship, the better. Her plan was to leave the house on the sly, and that meant going without any luggage. It seemed advisable to secure her cabin before using it for storage.

"Is there anything else I can do for you?" he asked.

There were a dozen things that had to be done. Her tilbury and team must be sold, for instance, but she would arrange that in her note to *Madrina*. Naturally he would ask a dozen questions if she did it before going.

"Nothing at the moment, thank you."

As he appeared to be making headway, Severn tried to push the reconciliation a step further. "Cousin, I am indeed sorry for my behavior these past days. We used to be . . . closer. I feel we are drifting apart."

His words conjured up the vast expanse of water that would soon separate them, and tears sprang unbidden into her eyes. She could not speak for the great lump in her throat. She just patted his hand, then turned and ran upstairs to pitch herself on her bed to cry.

What was the matter with her? Twice recently

she, who never cried, had been reduced to tears by Severn. Why should she cry over that horrid man? Yet at times he did not seem horrid. He could be quite sweet when he wanted. Surely she was not falling in love with him? Love was a joyful thing, not this awful ache at the heart. Severn was not at all the sort of man she meant to fall in love with. He was not gallant or jealous enough. Oh, but she feared she had fallen in love with him. Her heart quickened when he entered the room. Her flesh burned when he touched her. And to think of never seeing him again was like entering a dark, endless night.

She sensed that he wanted to marry her. Could she change him? What worse fate could a lady suffer than to love a husband who did not love her? Oh, he was gentleman enough to treat his wife with respect, but she wanted more than respect.

She wanted him to lose his head over her, to forget about propriety and money and just love her enough to make a fool of himself over her. She felt he was capable of that sort of passion if he would let himself go. He was jealous of Malvern, but it was a cold, English jealousy, which took itself out in words. A Spanish lover would have found an excuse for a duel. No, she would cut it off in one stroke, like a knife severing a thief's hand. It was the least painful thing in the long run, but in the near term, it was so very painful.

Chapter Twenty-two

Good to his word, Severn returned Helena's carriage and called off his bloodhound. She soon realized that even with her carriage, it was impossible to smuggle trunks out of the house, so she trimmed her luggage to a couple of large cases. Of course, Foster had no idea what was in the cases he carried to the *Princess Margaret*. The household knew Aylesbury had ordered jackets and assumed she had bought him other items of English fashion as well.

The days were busy with visits and callers, with parties in the evening, and especially with preparations for her ball. Early in the Season she had ordered a special gown for the occasion, of white tulle over a taffeta underskirt. As a prelude to her return to Spain, she meant to wear her hair in the Spanish style, lifted off her face with a comb high on the back of her head. She also meant to flout convention and wear a long, brightly colored Spanish shawl. What did she care if people talked? She would soon be away from their whispers.

Her relations with Severn continued to be coolly polite. He noticed in particular that she stiffened up at any mention of what she had been doing during the days when he was away. "I went driving," she would say in a chilly way that made any further question seem an imposition.

"How are you fixed for funds?" was also answered curtly.

"I shall repay you shortly, Severn, if that is what concerns you."

"That was not my meaning! Do you need more funds?"

"The money you were kind enough to advance me is more than sufficient. And how are things going at Whitehall?" always served as a diversion. He replied in detail, but it was perfectly obvious her interest was only perfunctory.

Helena was hardly more open with Lady Hadley. She feared she might betray her plan by a careless word. She did tell her godmother on Wednesday morning, however, that she planned to attend Moira's wedding that afternoon.

"You'll want an escort. Why not ask Severn to take you?"

"He is too busy, and besides he does not care for Moira."

"That won't bother Edward. He hardly ranted at Marion's engagement at all. You are having a good influence on him."

"I have no influence whatsoever on him."

Lady Hadley did not argue, but mentally she disagreed. Helena had had an influence, but it was not the influence she had expected. Edward was more considerate, gentler somehow, but he was not so carefree as he used to be. All that Whitehall business, for instance. And Helena's joie de vivre had left her entirely. She went through the motions of her Season as if it was a duty. She had expected fireworks from those two youngsters, but what they produced was a cold pudding.

Helena made a careful toilette for the wedding and felt horribly underdressed. The other guests, mostly Gagehot's friends and relatives, were arrayed in festive finery. It was a small, quiet ceremony. Helena listened to the fateful words of the wedding vows with awe. What a serious business it was. "Till death do us part." The couple were radiant with joy. They wore the same doting look that Marion and Malvern wore.

How did it come that those two couples, so much less fortunate than she and Severn in worldly circumstances, had found true love? Moira and Gagehot were old and well past their physical prime. Malvern was penniless and struggling to make his way in the world. Without undue vanity, Helena knew she was prettier than Marion, and, of course, wealthier. Yet with youth, attractiveness, and wealth, she had not found anyone to love her as these two ladies were loved.

She felt so depressed that she excused herself before the wedding feast and left, after wishing Moira and Gagehot every happiness. She stopped only to arrange to have a hansom cab meet her after her ball to take her to the ship. At home she read the social columns of the journal. Every second item was an engagement notice. All the ladies were nabbing *partis*.

At four she began listening for the sound of Severn's arrival. He often came home early and usually seemed in the mood for conversation. Perhaps she would oblige him today, tell him about Moira's wedding and reveal something of her feelings. For an hour she waited, then went to her room.

Severn arrived home barely in time to change for dinner. He did not think to ask what she had done that afternoon, and she didn't tell him. They attended three different routs that evening. Helena stood up with Severn at the first one, then avoided him. Rutledge had returned from Newmarket, and she obliged him with dances at two of the parties.

On the day before her own ball, a young lady was allowed to be on the fidgets. The next day Helena oversaw the placement of flowers and chairs and tried to make herself useful. The Comstocks called to see if they could be of service and remained for tea. Their talk was of Marion's nuptials. Every word pierced Helena like a thorn. She was invited to a ball in the evening but decided to remain at home.

Severn agreed at once. He welcomed this opportunity of privacy with her. Never before had he wooed in vain. Helena's lack of interest was a continuing frustration. It was a blow to his heart, as well as his pride. "An excellent idea," he said. "We shall have a quiet evening. You will want an early night, to be in looks for your own party."

"I have letters to write," she said, and went upstairs.

Knowing that tomorrow would be a busy day, she wrote her farewell note to Lady Hadley, to be placed on her pillow when she left. She gave effusive thanks for her godmother's hospitality and apologized for leaving so informally. When she tried to explain the reason for her flight, invention ran dry, so she said simply that it was for the best. Of course, she gave no clue that Spain was her destination. Perhaps they would think she had gone to Papa's estate in Lancashire. At the bottom she wrote a postscript for Severn, asking him to sell her tilbury and team and please to

201

take the hundred pounds she owed him from the sum. Then she counted her money. She had enough to leave pourboires for the servants.

As darkness fell, she sat at the window, watching the stars come out. A fat white moon floated over the chimney pots. Tomorrow night it would float over the ocean, but it would shine on both her and Eduardo, the only thing they shared.

Severn announced in the morning that he would not go into work that day. "You must!" she said. She could not bear a whole day with him at her shoulder. Her nerves were already on edge.

"Your ball is important to you, Cousin. I want nothing lacking to make it a happy occasion. I might be able to help."

She was touched at his thoughtfulness. For once he was actually putting her before his politics. "You have work to do. *Madrina* and I will be on hand if any difficulty arises."

"Are you sure?"

"Very sure, Eduardo."

His face eased into a smile. "You have not called me that for some time, Helena."

"I always call you that in my thoughts," she said.

He left, much cheered. This promised well for the evening. Before it was over, he hoped to make his proposal.

The coiffeur arrived at five to do the ladies' hair. At six he left, and Sally helped Helena into her new gown.

"You look like a bride," Sally said, surveying the vision of beauty before her—eyes sparkling, a flush lighting the youthful cheeks, and the exquisite gown of virginal white.

Sally took up the Spanish shawl and placed it around her mistress's shoulders before she descended the staircase. A few of the two dozen guests invited for dinner before the ball had already arrived. Severn was required to entertain them in the saloon. He did not see Helena until she appeared at the doorway in her Spanish hairdo, with the jeweled comb protruding at the top and her blazing shawl lending a splash of color. For a brief moment, he felt he had been pitched back a month, to the day of her arrival. The memory was like a jolt to his heart.

The little gasp from the others in the room told him Helena's toilette had not found favor. Blind idiots! He hastened forward, smiling, to greet her with a bow.

"Señorita, you look enchanting."

Conversation erupted in the saloon as curious eyes conned Helena. "I feared you might not like it," she said to Severn.

"A man would have to be a severe critic indeed to find a fault with—perfection. And you have already taken me to task for criticizing things I know so little of."

"I expect you know something about ladies' toilettes."

"I know what I like," he said, and led her into the room.

Severn, who was recognized as an authority in social matters, was used as a guide, and Helena's Spanish graces were accepted without further disapproval. She was half a foreigner, after all, and the gown was white, at least.

Neither Malvern nor Marion had any fault to find. Mrs. Comstock continued squinting, but when Malvern smiled, she was won over. They had sherry, and then Lady Hadley led the way into the dining room. The table was a marvel of crystal, silver, and roses. Lady Hadley had pulled out all the stops to put on a feast worthy of *Cousina*. Course followed by course, with many removes and much champagne.

It was a night whose memory any lady might treasure, but for Helena, it was salt in the wound. Severn was warmly attentive, but she would have preferred a touch of temper, to ease her parting. They opened the ball with the minuet, to a little spate of conjecture. If Severn was not wearing the smile of a bridegroom, they would be much surprised. Well, he might smile, beating the duke to the Spanish lady's fortune!

There was considerable speculation of this sort, even among the debs. Helena chanced to overhear one ill-natured lady explain the matter to a less informed friend when she slipped abovestairs a moment to rearrange her comb, which had shaken loose during a country dance. The ladies were unaware that Lady Helena was behind them on the broad staircase.

"It looks like a match for Severn," one lady mentioned.

"There was never any doubt of it, Cathy. Severn let a fortune like that slip through his fingers? Not likely."

"But Lady Helena is very pretty."

"She is handsome, I allow, but not quite comme il faut. That garish shawl she is wearing tonight, and her hair! Severn will trim her into line once they are married, of course. I don't envy her, myself. She'd have been better off with the duke. I wonder how Severn turned him off?"

"Did the duke make an offer?" Cathy asked.

"Who knows? Severn would not announce it, would he? Not until he has Lady Helena firmly in his pocket."

It was just the tonic Helena required to firm her

determination. She could not fool herself into thinking she was imagining Severn's true intentions, when they were common knowledge. She left off her shawl, as the young ladies seemed to think it inappropriate, but retained her Spanish comb when she went below to continue dancing the night away, while her heart throbbed angrily within her.

She wanted to cry but had to force smiles. A feverish gaiety seized her, and she danced and flirted outrageously with any young gentleman of a mind to oblige her. She made a special point to stand up twice with the duke, the second time for the waltzes. That set the gossips to chattering!

It also brought Severn to her side the instant the waltzes were finished. He took a firm grip on her elbow and led her from the floor. "Was it really necessary for you to make a spectacle of yourself?" he demanded.

"Spectacle? Surely a lady is allowed to waltz at her own ball, Severn."

"You stood up with him twice!"

"Perhaps as an indication of my intentions," she riposted.

His reply was hot and hasty. "Has he offered for you without asking my permission?"

"He is a duke of good character and vast fortune. You could not refuse him permission if he asked, so why argue?"

"Are you going to marry him?" he asked, his voice louder, his brow blacker, and his mood angrier.

"You will be the second to know if I accept an offer. It will be for my chaperon to give the duke permission. Stick to counting my pounds and pence, Severn. You are so good at that."

She strode angrily away and latched on to the

first gentleman she met. She would not satisfy Severn by running to her room and hiding. She heard scarcely a note of Juan's concert, though she was happy to hear the loud applause. Many matrons expressed an interest in hiring him. After the musical interlude, she danced until the last guest had left, at which time she thanked Lady Hadley effusively. As it was the last time she would see dear *Madrina*, she wrapped her arms around her.

"How shall I ever thank you for all you have done, *Madrina*? It was worth coming to England, just to meet you."

"We have enjoyed every minute of it. Haven't we, Edward?"

"It has been a great pleasure," he said, with a face like a martyr. "And now, as it is well past two o'clock, I suggest we all retire and continue our discussion in the morning."

"But before I go, I want to thank you, too, Severn," Helena said. She took a long look at him, storing up an image of this angry mood, which would do much in the days ahead to convince her she had acted wisely in fleeing. She reached out and shook his hand. He frowned in puzzlement but returned the handshake. Then Lady Helena turned and ran upstairs.

"She is worn out, poor child," Lady Hadley said.

Severn tried to convince himself it was fatigue that had caused Helena's strange mood—almost as if she were saying good-bye with that handshake.

Chapter Twenty-three

Sally had insisted on staying up till the small hours of the morning to assist her mistress to bed. Her ladyship looked so fagged that she did not press her for details as she removed the Spanish comb and brushed out her hair.

"It was lovely, Sally. My godmama has been so very kind to me. And you have been a model dresser. I want you to have this." She handed Sally the Spanish comb.

"Oh, miss! It's too much!" Sally said, but she snatched it eagerly.

"If you ever require a character, I shall be happy to give you one," Helena said.

"If you're that fond of me, your ladyship, why don't you take me with you?" She wondered why her mistress should blanch and stare at that hint. "When you marry, I mean."

"But I have no plan to marry in the near future."

"I'm amazed his lordship didn't come up to scratch. You'd have him, I fancy?" Sally peered into the mirror to see how this piece of impertinence was accepted. Lady Helena looked forlorn. "Lord Severn is so gone on you, the whole house is talking about it. We've never seen him so taken. Sits by the hour staring at the wall, Sugden says, with a

207

moonish look on his face. He's a good master. Lively but steady. 'He'll wear well,' my ma would say. You can't say better than that."

"He will make some lady a good husband. I find him cold."

"You're from Spain, your ladyship. He ain't cold for an Englishman. You could heat him up, I daresay, with encouraging." On this piece of wisdom she lay down her brush and went to turn down the bed. Over her shoulder she said, "You can tell me all about the party tomorrow, ma'am. What gents you danced with and all the naughty things they said. Now into bed with you."

"Run along to bed, Sally. You should not have stayed up so late, but I am happy you did." Those are the last words I shall ever say to my faithful servant, Helena thought.

As soon as Sally was gone, Helena put on her traveling suit. She placed the letter for *Madrina* on her pillow and arranged the servants' pourboires in discrete piles on her desk. She wrote a special thank-you note to Sally, then sat and waited for the household to settle down. It seemed an age before complete silence reigned. She opened the door a crack, looked, and listened. No sound came from the hallway. No light shone up from below. She crept out quietly and tiptoed down the front stairs, through the hall, and to the front door.

Its well-oiled hinges emitted no telltale squawk as she opened it. She was outside, with pale moonlight silvering the cobblestones. If all went according to plan, her hansom cab should be waiting around the corner at Chapel Street. Her feet flew over the cobblestones. She peered into the darkness and heard the whinny of the team before she spotted the carriage. Apparently the driver saw her, for the carriage suddenly lurched forward. Within a minute, it was beside her. "The docks," she said, and opened the door herself to enter.

Once inside the rumbling carriage, she relaxed against the leather squabs. The most harrowing part of her flight was accomplished. Now she had only to sit and wait until they reached the dock, board the ship, and wait again until the tide and winds were favorable for its departure. Wrapped in her own thoughts, she paid no heed to the squalid parts of the town the carriage traversed. When they drove past a strolling group of bucks, Helena hid herself, for the sight of a lone female within might incite them to mischief.

They hollered to the driver to stop, thinking the carriage was empty. The driver wisely urged his nags on to a trot and outran them. Nothing else of any account happened, and before long she was let down at the dockside. Seven ships rose up from the river, silhouetted against the silver sky. The fat moon's reflection bobbed on the shiny black water. Above, the sky was spangled with stars, promising good weather. She peered into the darkness to read the ships' names. "That one," she told the driver, pointing to the *Princess Margaret*.

The driver accompanied her to the ship, and she gave him his fare. "Thank you for your help, sir," she said.

He felt uneasy, leaving a lady alone at night in such a dangerous place. "I'll wait till you're taken aboard, milady."

The ship was in darkness, but a few shouts brought the night guard to the railing. The driver shouted her name, and the plank was let down. At last she was on board ship.

"When will we be setting sail?" she asked eagerly.

"Captain says by afternoon, ma'am, with the tide."

"That long!"

"Why don't you catch a few winks, your ladyship? 'Twill be morning soon enough. We might be off sooner, if we get a good western wind."

He led her to her cabin and lit the lamp. The cabin was similar to the one she had occupied during her trip to England. It was as comfortable as such a confined space could be, with a little bed in the corner, a set of drawers built in, and even a small desk. She saw her cases stowed at the end of the bed. She would unpack them tomorrow morning. She sank onto the bed, emotionally exhausted, and eventually fell into a fitful sleep.

When she awoke, a shaft of sunlight penetrated at the porthole window. The shriek of sea gulls mingled with the sound of human voices and the busy patter of sailors' feet as they went about their chores. She wanted to go up on deck but was wary of making herself visible, lest Severn discover her flight and come after her. He could not know where she had gone, but eventually he might guess. She should have left a note hinting him in some other direction. A runaway match occurred to her.

She ordered breakfast in her cabin. A full breakfast of gammon and eggs and toast and tea soon arrived. Food would be less satisfying toward the end of the trip, but while the ship was docked, fresh supplies were available. She ate desultorily, to pass the time. Eight-thirty. Five hours, even if they left as early as one-thirty in the afternoon.

At eight-thirty Severn was just rising after his late night. He would take the morning off from work and drive Helena into the countryside to explain away last night's temper. At nine he was in the breakfast parlor.

"Lady Helena is not up yet?" he asked the footman.

"No, sir. Not yet."

It was only to be expected. At nine-thirty he had finished a second cup of tea. He was about to go to his study to await Helena when Sugden appeared at the door, followed by a trembling Sally. "Tell him what you told me," Sugden ordered.

"She's gone, milord," Sally said, and burst into tears.

"What the devil is she talking about?" Severn demanded.

"It is her ladyship, milord. Lady Helena, that is to say. She is not in her room. Her bed has not been slept in. There is a note for ladyship, who has not arisen yet."

"Bring it to me at once!" Severn demanded.

Sugden had foreseen this demand and handed over the note. Severn tore it open and scanned it. He sat a moment, pale and distraught, trying to make sense of it. "She's gone," he said in a hollow voice.

"Yes, milord. Shall I have your carriage called?"

"Yes, have my curricle brought around at once." He turned to Sally. "Did she take her clothes with her?"

"No, sir. Not most of them. A few things are missing."

211

"Those cases ostensibly for Lord Aylesbury that her ladyship has been taking away ..." Sugden suggested, peering to see if he exceeded his authority.

"What cases? A couple of jackets do not require cases."

Sugden explained. Sally burst into a fresh shower of tears. "I had a funny feeling last night that something was amiss when she said she'd give me a character."

Severn recalled that he had had the same feeling when she said good-bye. He jumped up from the table and ran to his mother's room. He entered without knocking, waving the note. "Helena's gone, run away," he announced.

Lady Hadley, who had been enjoying a comfortable cup of tea while glancing through the court news, dropped her teacup. A brown stain spread over an antique, hand-embroidered silk quilt. "Good God!" she exclaimed. "Where could she be?"

"Rutledge!" Severn growled, and turned to pace from the room. Two dances last night, and that rallying challenge that the duke was "unexceptionable."

"I say, Edward!" his mama called. "If it is Rutledge, why make a runaway match? No one could possibly object to him."

"That mawworm! *I* object!" Severn howled, and fled downstairs to pace and curse until his curricle arrived.

He drove straight to Berkeley Square, where an astonished Rutledge received him. That the duke was at home, calmly eating a beefsteak, told Severn he was mistaken. He disliked to reveal

Helena's outrageous behavior, but the duke came to his own conclusions.

"Done a flit, has she? You must have offered for her, Severn. Can't think what else would send her flying off."

"She didn't say anything to you last night?"

"Nothing of any account. I wonder who the lucky fellow is. Try the Great North Road, my friend. If she's scampered on you, she must be headed for Gretna Green. May I join in the search?"

"No," Severn said baldly. "And I don't want this story whispered about town, Duke. If I hear one word—"

"The only word you shall hear from me is *mum*."

Severn's next notion was to hunt down Malvern. That engagement to Marion was dust in his eyes. He had run off with Helena. Severn had no notion where Malvern lived, but he knew where he worked, at least, and went to Whitehall. He found Malvern in his office, scribbling at a desk.

"Where is she?" Severn demanded.

Malvern glanced up in confusion. "She and Mrs. Comstock planned to visit Bond Street this morning, I believe. Why—"

"I don't mean Marion. What have you done with Helena?"

"Helena? What the deuce are you talking about?" Confusion soon rose to amusement. "Has she run off on you, Severn?" He was surprised she had executed her threat so swiftly.

"Certainly not! And if you tell a single soul—"

"Have you not heard, Severn? I am a reformed character. As you and I will soon be connections—grim thought, eh?—naturally I wish to brush all the family scandals under the carpet." He leaned

213

back, pondering. "I wonder . . ." He wanted to give Severn a clue without breaking faith with Helena.

"What is it?" Severn asked eagerly.

"I was just thinking—those Spanish folks at El Cafeto. You don't think she might have gone to them? I saw her talking to that guitar player, Juan, at the party last night," he said, as it occurred to him she might be waiting there until the ship was ready to sail.

"That's it! That's where she is! Thank you, Malvern."

He pounded back to his curricle, and after some driving in circles, finally found El Cafeto. Juan was not there, but after some confused bilingual conversation, half of which he could not understand, he was directed to the set of rooms across the street where Juan lived. He ran across the street, up the narrow, dark stairs, and pounded at the indicated door.

Juan replied at once, wearing a gleaming smile. "Milord! You have another party for me to play, yes? I was a very success at Lady Helena's ball. All the world—"

Severn pushed him aside and barged into the apartment. He rushed through the few rooms, a kitchen and bedroom, and could see quite clearly that she was not there. Nothing indicated she had ever been there.

"What you are looking for, please?" Juan asked.

"Lady Helena. Have you seen her?"

"But yes!"

"Where?" The word came out like a bark.

"At her party. Very beautiful, all in white."

"Have you seen her since then?"

"But no, milord. She is missing person?"

214

"No," Severn said, as he did not wish to waste time explaining and was convinced Juan was telling the truth.

He went once again to his curricle. Anxiety pinched like a vice at his chest. Where had she gone? A lady did not disappear into thin air. She had apparently not sought the assistance of any of her friends. Perhaps Marion knew something. But Marion was shopping on Bond Street. It would be like looking for a needle in a haystack, but as nothing else occurred to him, he drove there and continued driving up and down the street at a dangerous pace until he spotted Marion and Mrs. Comstock coming out of a drapery shop. He leapt from his rig, leaving it unattended, and darted up to them.

"Marion, Helena has run away," he said. "Did she say anything to you last night? I've been all over . . . to Malvern. . . ."

Marion reminded herself that Helena had not said anything *last night*. If Malvern was not telling, neither was she. She and Mrs. Comstock expressed the proper amount of shock and concern but were of no help at all in solving the problem.

"I knew she was after Malvern," Mrs. Comstock said, with a spiteful smile. "When she saw it was hopeless, she took to her heels. The Spaniards are famous for their pride, you must know, Severn. She would not take defeat lightly."

"Don't be so foolish," he said, and stormed back to his curricle.

Invention failed him. He could think of nowhere else to look, and in desperation he drove home, nurturing the forlorn hope that she had returned. Sugden's worried face told him she had not, but he asked anyway. "She didn't come back?"

"No, milord. No word. Her ladyship is most anxious to speak with you. She is in the morning parlor."

He found his mother there, pacing to and fro in front of the window. "No word?" she asked. Severn just shook his head and gave a brief description of his morning.

"It is so unlike *Cousina*," she said. "She was always so thoughtful. There is nothing for it but to call in Bow Street, then. We cannot hope to scour all of London ourselves. Indeed she has probably left London. Gone into the country to hide, or back to Spain." Severn gave her a sharp look. "But no," she said, "she would not have left without telling me. I doubt she had enough cash to pay for her passage. I know she was short."

"She borrowed a hundred pounds from me," Severn said. "Now I know why she would not tell me what she wanted it for."

"It was a wedding gift for Mrs. Petrel-Jones. She married Gagehot on Wednesday. Helena attended the wedding."

"Why did you not tell me?" he demanded.

His mama's patience broke and she turned on her son. "Because you always make such a business of nothing, just like your papa. You would have jawed at her. Besides, it was none of your business. She always told *me* what she was up to, just as she should. If you were not so swift to judge, we would have told you as well. I place this whole affair in your dish, Edward. Anyone could see the poor child *wanted* to love you, but you would not let her."

"Mama, how can you say such a thing!" he exclaimed, deeply shocked. "My whole aim since the

216

first moment I laid eyes on her was to win her. I am sick with love."

"You concealed it well. It looked more like temper to me."

"Now I've lost her forever," he said, staring with grim fortitude into the cold grate.

His mama's maternal instincts were touched. "She doesn't love anyone else, Son. Can you not follow her to Spain?"

Severn looked at her in consternation. "Go to Spain?"

"Where else can she have gone?"

"She would not leave all her pretty clothes behind if she were going to Spain."

"Oh, pooh! Stop thinking like a man, Edward. Besides, she took a few cases out of the house."

You always think when you should feel, Helena had said to him. But he needed head as well as heart now. She had been reading the marine schedule in the library the other day. He turned and hurried to the library.

A pile of recent journals was stacked at one end of the table. He began rooting through them. Sugden came and inquired if his lordship would like a bite of lunch, as it was one o'clock. Severn raised his hand and batted Sugden away, without lifting his eyes from the papers. He flipped pages quickly, until his eye caught the pen markings Helena had made. *Princess Margaret*, bound for Spain—and the date was today! He glanced at his watch. She might already have left! How she must hate him, to have done this. It was all his fault. He had nagged at the poor girl until, in desperation, she had fled his house.

He must get her back. Perhaps he could find a

217

fast ship to overtake the *Princess Margaret*. He hastened back to his rig and whipped his grays to sixteen miles an hour, narrowly avoiding collision with Sir Isaac Morton's brougham and very nearly running down various innocent pedestrians on the way. Fists were shaken and voices raised as he weaved his way through London's busy traffic.

She had left her tilbury behind to repay his debt. The debt that he had chided her for so severely, and it was only a gift to her papa's lightskirt, after all. She was determined to do the right thing if Aylesbury was not. He saw a ship drawing anchor as he reached the dock. As he drew closer, the words *Princess Margaret* could be seen through the mist. The ship was drawing ever farther away. He leapt down and ran to the dock. On the stern of the deck a group of passengers waved. He espied a lone female figure set a little apart from the others. Helena! Her shoulders sagged forlornly. Then they straightened, and an arm rose. "Severn! Eduardo!" The echo of her voice flew over the water to pierce his heart.

"Helena! Darling!" he called, to the amusement of the dockworkers and people come to see a friend off. "I love you."

Her hands rose to her lips. A smile beamed through her tears. "I am coming back!" she called.

"No, don't jump!"

Helena turned and left the deck.

Severn stood, undecided. Knowing her impetuosity, he feared she meant to jump overboard. He looked at the ship, trying to gauge its distance from shore and its speed. It was not so very far. He could swim a little. He looked down at the roiling, treacherous waters, and his heart froze. He who hesitates is lost. Without further thought, he plunged into the water, feet first. The deep, dark, cold waves closed over him and he went down, down, until he thought he would never rise again. When he finally bobbed back to the surface, he began trying to splash his way toward the ship. Great waves rose up to inundate him. His boots filled with water, and his sodden clothes dragged him down.

"Gorblimey!" a dockworker exclaimed, and tossed him a cork float. Severn grabbed on to it and found it kept him afloat. By gripping it between his hands and kicking, he made some headway, but he could not seem to get any nearer the ship. He felt an utter fool and was about to abandon his quixotic quest when he saw a small rowboat coming toward him. One sailor was at the oars, and standing at the prow like a Valkyrie carving come to life was Helena, waving furiously. He could not make out whether she was laughing or crying.

When the small boat had drawn alongside, the sailor hauled him aboard, very nearly capsizing the boat in the process. Helena threw her arms around him. "Eduardo! How gallant!" she said, laughing through her tears. "You *do* love me! Why could you not have told me sooner?"

"I have loved you to distraction for weeks. And don't you dare laugh at me, you wretch!" he said, crushing her against his soaking body for a ruthless kiss. A loud roar of approval rose up from the throng on the dock. Word of his folly was bound to reach society's ears. Lord Severn, jumping into the Thames and trying to outrun a frigate, for the sake of love. Some chancellor he would make! He pushed the thought aside.

Helena drew back and gazed lovingly at him.

"Oh, Eduardo, you were *magnífico*," she murmured. "Never will I forget it. You risked certain death for me, and I thought you were cold."

"I *am* cold," he said as a shiver seized him.

"So English, ignoring praise. I shall try very hard to become accustomed to your restrained ways."

"Don't you dare change," he said, squeezing her fingers. "I love you just as you are. Of course, you must marry me at once, to save my reputation."

"Of course," she said dreamily. "You will wear a bordeaux jacket with Mechlin lace."

"Why not?" He laughed. "Why not?" He sensed that his new life would not be quite so settled as he had feared, and he was heartily grateful. But for her, he might have become Papa. Now he was a gallant, in love with and loved by the most beautiful lady in England. Why should he not wear a bordeaux jacket, if it would please her?

Helena put her hand trustingly in his. "I did not think you would come, but I hoped right till the last minute."

He lifted her hand to his lips and kissed it, too happy to find words.